The stories of Calum the island policeman at last collected together as a book.

A law unto himself and the bane of the Inspector's life, Calum's spirited adventures from the West Highlands and Islands lend a new and hilarious perspective to law n'order.

Willie Robertson saw active service as a policeman in Greenock and various stations in Argyll. His last posting before retirement was in Carradale. He now lives on the Mull of Kintyre.

Calum's Way of It!

Willie Robertson

dedicated to all the unseen heroines
of single man police stations

First published 1995
Argyll Publishing
Glendaruel
Argyll PA22 3AE
Scotland

Acknowledgements are due to *The Scots Magazine*
where The Colonel was first published. Also to the
Strathclyde Guardian, the magazine for Strathclyde
police where many of the other stories and some
illustrations were first published.

British Library Cataloguing-in-Publication Data.
A catalogue record for this book is available from
the British Library.

ISBN 1874640 75 0

Origination
Cordfall Ltd, Glasgow

Printing
Martins the Printers, Berwick upon Tweed

contents

1

Calum takes the Oath

Calum McKinnon had the singular good fortune to be born a Scot, and not just any Scot, but a Highland Scot. The language of the Gael was native to him and the adventures of Cu-Chullin and the Fingalians real to his child's imagination. With his two elder brothers, he snared rabbits on the heather hills which overlooked his father's croft, close by the shores of the Firth of Lorn, fished the lochans and streams for the speckled trout, and by moonlight, netted the sandy sea-bays of the rocky coast for the silver salmon in their season.

    That the Great Ones of his native land would have viewed such natural pursuits as an infringement of their landed rights, never occurred to him. He had heard his parents talk of The Laird but who, or what manner of man he was, he had no idea.

What the men of the house brought home, his mother cooked and served and, if this Laird had come hungry to their door, he would have received *Ceud mile failte* and a place at the table. Of that Calum had no doubt.

At the little school some four miles walk from the croft Calum was taught to read and write in English and, within the confines of the school and playground, converse in that language. He learned something of the world beyond his immediate glens and that, contrary to his earlier belief, he was not descended from mystical Celtic heroes but from an illiterate tribe of savages. These had been salvaged, he was taught, from the abyss of ignorance by courtesy of the English language and a benevolent government seated far to the south of his home.

A Lowlander by birth, Calum's teacher made it evident that he did not look for intellectual brilliance in his pupils. A tenuous grasp of the three Rs and an unquestioning respect for the authority of their "betters" would suffice from the cradle to the grave. Any inclination to quest learning beyond these limits would be presumption.

A doubtless genetic inheritance from his savage ancestors resulted in Calum leaving school at the age of fourteen with an unquestioning respect for the three Rs, but only a tenuous grasp of the requirement to bow to the authority of his "betters". This perversion of the teacher's philosophy was to endure throughout his life and cause him no end of bother.

One by one, the McKinnon boys were called up to the war—the two elder brothers to the Royal Navy and Calum, in the last years, to the army. When hostilities ceased, all three returned home, and in one piece. Historically, the fate of younger sons, rich and poor alike, has been to seek their fortunes beyond the parental walls and the McKinnons were no exception. Service in the navy had given Calum's second brother itchy feet and within a month he was back at sea again on a wandering freighter. The oldest settled to the work of the croft, as was expected of him. And Calum? Well, he was somewhat at a loss.

For a time he worked about the place mending the roof, gathering the sheep off the hill for the dipping and repairing the dry-stone dyke round the fank. But increasingly he recognised that he was not really needed.

"I'm going off to Oban, for a spell," Calum announced one morning. "There should be plenty of work there and good money, I'm thinking. I'll put up at Auntie Katie's till I see what's doing." And so, with a few necessities packed in his army haversack, Calum hiked it to the main road and caught the bus to the bustling fishing port of Oban.

It didn't take him long to discover he had been unduly optimistic regarding the likelihood of finding employment in that town. As elsewhere in the country, there was no shortage of young men returned from the war to a land ill-prepared for heroes to live in. Berths on fishing-boats were at a premium, forestry workers ten a penny and railway jobs booked up for generations to come. All Calum seemed to have going for him were a sturdy frame and a pair of broad shoulders. With these assets, he earned casual money humping bags of coal up tenement stairs and stacking boxes of fish on the pier.

Late one bitterly cold November evening, Chance decided to take a hand in Calum's affairs. On a windswept deserted pier he was scrubbing and hosing down the day's empty whitefish boxes when, beyond his view in the darkness, he heard raised voices. This in itself was not unusual in a harbour filled with trawlers and skiffs from all parts of the country and abroad. As he worked on unconcerned he easily identified the disruptants as two foreigners, Dutch or maybe German. It was only when the shouting gave way to blows that Calum laid down the hose and strolled round the stow of boxes to observe the entertainment.

By the diffused glimmer of the harbour lights he saw not two but three men. Two of them dressed in fisherman's gear were being pulled apart, with some difficulty, by a dice-capped police sergeant. Fists were still flailing and as the sergeant was stationed between the contestants he was receiving more than a fair share of the punches.

Calum could not but be impressed by the self-control shown by the policeman under extreme provocation. Although the odds were against him, it was apparent to Calum that the lawman was rapidly gaining the upper hand and that the two would soon be sleeping it off in a nice warm cell. He almost envied them for his work was no where nearly finished and it was exceedingly cold.

But just as Calum was about to return to his labours, a figure with a bottle grasped in its upraised hand, detached itself from the shadows and lunged in the direction of the sergeant's unprotected back. Calum had never played rugby-football but the flying-tackle with which he brought down the intruder would have lifted the roof off the Murrayfield stadium.

The sergeant who had just succeeded in snapping the handcuffs on his by then subdued prisoners, jerked round as the bottle shattered behind him. Calum had the attacker's left arm screwed up behind him and his head pulled hard back by the hair as he raised him effortlessly from the ground.

"No sense of fair play, these foreigners," Calum grinned by way of explanation, nodding in the direction of the smashed bottle. "What will I do with him?"

"You can bring him along to the station for me if you

will. I've only got two hands and I'm needing both of them as you can see," was the reply.

At the police station, Calum was relieved of his prisoner and a statement taken from him by a young constable. The paper work completed, he was on the point of leaving when the sergeant detained him. "Come on down to the canteen," he invited. "We could both do with a cup I'm thinking."

It was pleasantly warm in the canteen, the tea strong and sweet to Calum's taste, and the meat sandwich from the sergeant's piece-box substantial, like the man himself. His host was so skilled at his trade that without realising he was being pumped, Calum related to him his entire history.

When his tale had run its course, Calum glanced at the clock on the wall. "*Mo creach*, Sergeant, just look at the time that's in it. I'll need to get back to work."

"The way I see it," the sergeant mused, refilling the tea mugs, "a man who can handle himself as you did tonight could do better for himself than washing fish boxes for a living." He stirred his tea thoughtfully. "He could try for the police, for instance. There's always openings, but for the right kind of man, you'll understand."

"The Police," Calum echoed, startled at the very idea. "Och, but is there not examinations on paper and the likes to be sat and myself is not scholar."

"Schooling's no bad thing," the sergeant admitted. "But in a tight spot, like tonight, it's quick thinking and a strong right arm that's needed."

The sergeant rose to his feet. "Finish your tea. I'll be right back." He returned moments later with some printed sheets of paper which he handed to Calum. "That's an example of the exam you'd be taking. I'm sure there's nothing there that would flummox you. Come back here tomorrow at 2 o'clock and have a go at it, lad. The Superintendent will be away for the day—which will be no bad thing," he judged. "I'll be supervising the examination and Inspector McLean will be doing the marking. We joined the Force together, the Inspector and I, and understand each other just fine."

The sergeant accompanied Calum to the front door. As they were parting, he said. "There are three possible answers to any question—the wrong one, the right one and . . . the near as dammit one. As I said before, the Inspector and I have a fine understanding. Don't be late tomorrow."

The following day Calum sweated through the examination under the eye of the sergeant, then passed an agonising hour seated in the front office awaiting the result.

"You've passed," the sergeant congratulated, extending a large horny hand. "Welcome to the Force, lad."

With the relief that he felt, Calum didn't think to ask the segeant if the "fine understanding" between himself and the Inspector had played any part in the day's business and the sergeant didn't think to tell him.

Calum had to go through the training at the Police College and in the years that followed he spent time at most mainland police stations throughout the County of Argyll.

Oddly, the stirring qualities that the sergeant had observed in him that night on Oban pier were decidedly indiscernible to his office-bound superiors with the result that he was regularly paraded before inspectors and superintendednts to explain the meagre number of charge sheets, bearing his signature, passing across their desks.

Calum's native ability to amicably settle most of his day's police problems without taking out his notebook was apparently not what was required of him by career-minded higher ranks who looked to work-horses like Calum to expedite their ascent of the promotional ladder. This disinclination to actively assist in the ways of his "betters" meant that his stay in any station or division of the force was as temporary as the officer in charge could reasonably make it, without attracting the unwanted attention of the Chief Constable.

Dictatorships have the distinct advantage of having two methods of ridding themselves of the undesirables—the firing-squad or enforced banishment to the uttermost regions. Democracies, on the other hand, are restricted to the latter course, and even then without the element of force. Since a dawn march to the brick wall and the blindfold was out of the question, Calum's deportation was to a one-man island police-station.

2

A Tale of a Tail

In the tiny police office, the telephone sounded. With the authority entrusted to him by an enlightened government, the enforcer of the laws of the land on this remote seabound West Highland corner of Her Britannic Majesty's historic realm was Constable Calum McKinnon.

Of middle years and average height, he had quickly learned to employ the pacific arts of patience, understanding, a calm demeanour and an open mind rather than the miriad Acts of Parliament to maintain the Queen's Peace among his proud and well proportioned islanders. And with remarkable success.

As a result of this almost unique approach to his responsibilities, the authorities were put to little expense in supplying him with stationery and typewriter ribbons. And the single cell, furnished to house offenders, provided excellent storage space for his gardening tools.

The persistent ringing of the telephone brought Calum's wife Jean hurrying from her kitchen to the office, drying her hands on her apron before lifting the receiver.

"*An tusa a tha'nn a Shine. A bheil Calum aig an tigh?*" She recognised the voice of Seoras McLeod the piermaster and, being a Lewis woman herself, had no difficulty in understanding his sing-song accented Gaelic which was the cause of much head shaking among the local born islanders. These, rightly or wrongly, considered their own liquid syllables a perfect reproduction of Adam's speech in the Garden of Eden.

"No Seoras," she replied to his enquiry if her husband was at home. "He's out at the moment. Is anything wrong?"

"Nothing to distress yourself about, *a ghraidh-se*," Seoras assured her, "It's just that I saw a police inspector, in uniform, coming off the ferry this morning and myself was thinking that Calum should be knowing about it."

Hardly had Jean replaced the receiver than the office bell sounded and on opening the door she was confronted by the figure of Inspector Twatt, Calum's superior from the mainland, in full regalia.

"Good morning, Mrs McKinnon," he greeted as he pressed past her into the office noting, with satisfaction, Calum's absence from his place of duty. "Your husband appears to be out, or perhaps . . . eh . . . still in bed?" he added lightly watching her closely for the slightest sign of anxiety. No, her face betrayed nothing. He hadn't really expected to find McKinnon still between the sheets. Such good fortune, he knew from experience, seldom came his way.

"I don't think he was expecting you, Mr Twatt," Jean said, wishing that her husband would return.

"Oh," the inspector registered what he hoped would appear to be a genuine surprise. "Didn't he receive a telephone

15

call this morning to say that I'd be coming over to inspect his station?"

"No—I don't think so," she replied a little uncertainly. Her answer didn't surprise the inspector in the least as he had left specific instructions with Sergeant Scobie, a reliable man, to ensure that on no account was McKinnon to be advised beforehand of the intended visit.

"Really, Mrs McKinnon," he sighed, "if I don't attend to things myself they simply don't get done. If I had my way there would be a number of changes in this force." The thought gave him considerable satisfaction as he mentally placed the good lady's husband at the head of his list of changes.

The inspector leafed through and initialed the various official books to be found in the office, but his mind wasn't on the business. The man McKinnon was insufferable. If his living had to depend on commission earned from the reports he'd submitted, he'd have starved years ago.

There were many things that vexed the inspector. The failure of his superiors to appreciate his undoubted worth rankled. That buffoon, Anderson, now a chief inspector at headquarters and hadn't he run circles round him at the training college? It certainly wasn't brains that got him where he was. The inspector smiled knowingly. Funny how Anderson had been promoted only three months after marrying the County Convener's daughter. Coincidence? He knew better. And then there were the inadequates he had to work with, like Sergeant Scobie. Oh yes, he could trust him—a crawler if ever there was one. Such men disgusted him but, they did have their uses. Yes, and Superintendent Smith, his own superior back on the mainland. He couldn't rightly make that one out. A superintendent—and hardly out of the college. Some sort of a prodigy they must have considered him but he, Inspector Twatt, was yet to be convinced.

The inspector closed the report file on the desk before him and drummed his fingers on the polished surface. He'd have the last laugh yet, by thunder he would, or his name wasn't Hugh Twatt.

From Jean he learned that she had last seen her husband walking in the direction of the river and, as poachers had been active lately, this was probably his destination.

"Try the minister's pool, just beyond the bridge," she advised as he set off at a brisk pace.

As the inspector neared the bridge he became more wary and approached the parapet with caution. If the river was being poached it was more than likely McKinnon himself was the culprit. The possibility excited him.

Removing his cap he carefully raised his head above the parapet wall. His heart missed several beats as his eyes widened to take in the scene before him.

Constable Calum McKinnon, bare legged, his uniform trousers rolled up to the knees, his cap stuck jauntily on the back of the head, was standing calf deep in the dark waters of the pool, the fishing rod in his hands bent almost double as he held the strain against a hooked salmon thrashing the water some six yards away from him.

"McKinnon," the inspector yelped in a delirium of happiness as he vaulted over the parapet, slithered down the grassy bank and arrived at the water's edge.

Calum, hearing his name called, spared a hurried glance behind him then returned his full attention to controlling the fish. The inspector, his eyes feverishly bright, stood on the banks, hands on hips, master of the situation, glorious in his triumph.

"McKinnon, drop that rod *immediately* and report to me."

Considering the elation which was coursing through the inspector's whole being his voice was a model of restraint.

"I'll be with you in just a moment, Inspector," Calum replied over his shoulder. "If I give him line now, he'll be off downstream before you can wink."

"I said *immediately*, McKinnon, and that is an order. Drop it."

Calum hesitated for only a second then, resigned, he released his grip on the rod. It shot from his fingers like an arrow from a bow as the salmon, sensing its adversary's moment of indecision, hurled itself with all its remaining strength, into the white foam at the neck of the pool and disappeared in the tumult of water downstream, towing the rod and line in its wake.

Slowly Calum turned to face the inspector, puzzled how the loss of a good fish and an expensive rod could afford the man such undisguised pleasure. He had often been baffled in the past by his superior's commands but had always obeyed them to the best of his ability. He responded to an inborn belief in the need for discipline and the recognition that somewhere, somehow, someone in authority had observed qualities in the man which consistently escaped his notice.

The inspector swelled his lungs prior to executing the ultimate, verbal annihilation of Constable Calum McKinnon. A holocaust that would encompass being from his place of duty, idling his time and—joy beyond description—the illegal taking of game fish, a criminal charge.

"What the devil's happened, Calum?" The voice came from upstream.

The inspector's head jerked round. Nothing and no one was going to steal this moment from him.

A rotund figure in waders, waterproof jacket and deerstalker hat, carrying a landing net, lumbered towards them from behind the bushes on the opposite bank. The inspector's cup was near to over-flowing. McKinnon and an accomplice and he had them both, red handed.

"Stay right where you are, my man. My constables have you surrounded," the inspector lied, adding as an inspired afterthought, "there's no escape. I recognise you."

"Do you, Inspector? Do you, indeed. I am most gratified." The voice which issued from the barrel-like figure was not the expected whine of a felon caught in the act, but the rolling thunder of a three-decker's broadside. Dismissing the inspector's presence, as the great Admiral himself would have done a powder boy on the quarter-deck of his ship, the arrival addressed himself to Calum. "The fish, Calum, my rod . . . what happened to them?"

"I'm truly sorry, sir,"

Calum's appearance of utter dejection as he stood, head bowed, in the pool was wonderful to behold. "I was about to explain to the inspector that I was just holding your rod till you fetched your net, but he ordered me to drop it, immediately. Not a man to be trifled with, the inspector, sir. I had to obey."

Calum raised his head and, as he turned his gaze downstream, even the most casual observer couldn't fail to notice the solitary glistening tear which rolled from his cheek to add its mite to the river's volume. "Och, but its the grand fish he was to be sure, sir. And him half way to the sea by now . . . aye and your fine rod with him, I'm thinking."

Following the dialogue in silence, his eyes darting from one to the other, Inspector Twatt was conscious of the first niggling doubts as to the completeness of his victory. The accomplice was like no poacher he had met before and he'd dealt with a good many in his time—skulking, devious fellows who spoke in whispers. This one showed no fear of the inspector's presence and patently no urgent desire to melt into the undergrowth.

The tiny pinpricks of doubt and puzzlement which had been irritating the inspector changed, in an instant, to spear thrusts of mind-numbing horror. He watched the waterproofed figure advance with the ponderous irresistable action of an armoured tank. It went to the edge of the opposite bank, snatch off the deer-stalker, hurl it to the ground and expose to his stunned gaze the ominously glowering features of his acutely displeased Chief Constable.

"I . . . . I didn know it was your rod, sir," the inspector was floundering. "I thought it was McKinnon's. I thought he was poach . . ." his voice strangled to a stop as his dust dry throat contracted.

"You thought?" the Chief Constable's tone was flat, menacing. "Thinking is a process of which you are apparently incapable, Inspector Twatt."

An intolerable silence followed as the Chief Constables' withering stare devoured the now wilting form of the inspector, body and soul.

Calum paddled discreetly to the bank and having dried his feet with the spotless white handkerchief that his wife insisted on him carrying, pulled on his socks and boots.

"My rod will not retrieve itself, Inspector," the Chief Constable's voice, unchanged, broke the silence.

"Ah, no, just so, sir," the inspector stammered. Then in a bid to retain the remnants of his dignity and, hopefully his career, he turned to Calum, now dry footed and booted.

"You heard the Chief Constable. Quickly, McKinnon, back into the river. The rod can't have gone that far."

"I'm afraid," interposed the Chief Constable, "I require

the services of Constable McKinnon to drive me to the home of the Lord Lieutenant, where I'm expected for lunch."

The inspector directed a glance of the purest malevolence at Calum who, seemingly unaware of the inspector's discomfort, was conducting an examination of his finger nails with praiseworthy thoroughness.

As the inspector untied his shoelaces his eyes followed with loathing the course of the peat-darkened waters of the river as it leaped and tumbled downstream among the glass smooth rocks and half submerged treetrunks, his spirit daunted by the hopelessness of the task before him.

"Come, come, Inspector, we haven't time for such niceties," the bass rumble of the Chief Constable's voice spanned the intervening space. "I believe I see the butt-end jammed between those two rocks, there, just to the right of midstream."

Clutching at a last, faint hope of salvaging something of his future, the inspector's stockinged feet and immaculately pressed uniform trousers entered the murky waters of the shallows. Struggling to keep his balance against the rushing current, he was soon thigh-deep in the swirling surge of the central run.

The Chief Constable, having forded the river in his studded waders, stood by Calum observing the inspector's antics with mounting impatience.

"Quickly, Inspector," he bellowed, in a tone which doubtless he regarded as one of encouragement. "I can't keep his Lordship waiting for lunch all day."

Spurred by the spectre of demotion or even dismissal should he fail in his mission, the inspector lunged forward to grasp the now clearly visible butt of the rod, lost his footing and disappeared from sight in an upsurge of foam and spray, to reappear triumphantly holding aloft the errant fishing rod.

As he scrambled to the bank and dripped his way to the presence of the Chief Constable, his silver-braided hat set off downstream on a journey which, if unimpeded, would take it eventually to the shores of the New World.

"It seems to be undamaged," pronounced the Chief Constable, testing the rod for whip, grip and dip. "But it's not much use withour the reel, is it, Inspector?"

"The reel, sir," the inspector echoed weakly.

"The reel," the Chief Constable repeated with infinite patience. "The thing that holds the line, Inspector. It's missing."

The awful implication of his superior's statement registered in the mind of the now shivering frame of Inspector Twatt. This caused him, in the deep dark recess of his immortal soul, to curse his twenty-three years' loyal sevice to the force, with two more to go to pensionable age.

"I've been invited to fish General Semple's stretch this evening. Should be good for a sea-trout of two, I'd say," confided the Chief Constable, as he eased off his waders. "Drop the reel off at Constable McKinnon's house when you find it, Inspector. He can bring it when he picks me up tonight."

With a wave of the hand the Chief Constable set off up the path towards his car with Constable Calum McKinnon positioned at a respectful pace behind him.

"What do you fancy tonight, Calum?" the Chief Constable enquired. "A Grouse and Claret? No—perhaps not. A Teal and Silver—eh? That should do the trick, don't you think?"

As the car's engine note faded into the distance, Inspector Twatt's stockinged feet squelched their return journey to the water's edge, hesitated for a moment, then disappeared once more beneath its rippled surface.

3

Something of a Calum-ity

With the summer sun at its meridian, in a cloudless sky, Constable Calum McKinnon and his good friend, Roderick McPherson, minister of the parish, laid aside their rods. Finding shade beneath a tree by the riverbank they sat side by side, drawing contentedly on their pipes.

In the course of their conversation, the Minister touched on the subject of salmon-poaching, and the harm it did to the sport of angling. To his surprise, Calum's concurrence with this view was less than wholehearted.

To be sure, he condemned absolutely the plundering of rivers by netting and poisoning, but it was his opinion that there might be occasions when benefit of a general rather than an individual nature could result from the taking of a few fish without, strictly speaking, lawful authority.

For a time the Minister considered this unexpected response from someone dedicated to the maintainance of Law and Order.

"Could you, perhaps from your own experience, Calum, give me an example of such an occasion?" he asked, adding, "in strict confidence, of course."

With this assurance, Calum rested his back against the trunk of the tree and refilled his pipe.

"Some years ago, Roddy," he began, "I was stationed in a fishing village on the way between Oban and Fort William. *A dhia*, but it's a hard way to make a living, fishing the herring, and with little to show for it at the end of the day."

Calum weighed his next words carefully. "Suppose, out there on the sea, in the dark of night, and in circumstances never before experienced, the chance to make a real wage presented itself—Heaven sent you might say—would it be at all surprising if a skipper were tempted to think that the hand of Providence was in it? Like when Himself told the disciples where to cast their nets to fill them to bursting?"

He glanced mischievously at his companion. However, as the Minister showed no inclination to be drawn into a theological debate, Calum proceeded to relate a sequence of events. These began late one evening when the ring-net fishing-boat, Eriskay Lass cast off from the quay accompanied by her neighbour boat. They set course for the hunting grounds of the Minch.

Riding the swell of a rising tide, the Eriskay Lass lay, hove to, the solid menace of the coastal cliffs towering scarce a couple of hundred yards astern. By the glare of arc-lamps, the crew of four hauled the net, wet and heavy, across the tilting gunwale. On frantic wings, a ceiling of sea-gulls hovered, screeching in anticipation of the herring which should soon spill onto the wooden deck. In a flurry of oilskins and slithering sea-boots, crewmen from the neighbour boat leaped onboard as both vessels closed momentarily, then parted. Heaving together on the net they saw, relecting from below the surface, the first glint of living silver.

"Bring her in steady, boys," the cautionary voice of Angus John McLellan, the skipper of the boat, sounded from the dim interior of the wheelhouse. "That's the way, canny now, Archie."

Suddenly, as by common consent, the labouring figures froze. Holding the strain of the net, they peered, as if mesmerised, at the sea below them.

"What's happened . . . have we had a tearing?The crews reacted instantly to the bellow from the wheelhouse, bending in unison, as the remainder of the net was dragged aboard.

The boots of the men disappeared under a cascade that shimmered across the deck. Angus John, his eyes large as saucers in his tanned face, stared at the scene before him, the boat rocking below his feet, the wind sighing through the mast-stays. Sheening, like silver plate in a jeweller's show-case, not herring, but prime salmon on the homeward run, the flavour of the rain-swollen river already in the gills, threshed and flailed in the confines of the slippery deck—a cargo which, if untimely detected, could prove no less damning to the possessor than hogsheads of brandy.

"What ails you?" Angus John found his voice. "Into the hold with them, lads. Look lively now." Cupping his hands round his mouth, he hailed the skipper of his neighbour boat. "Come across, Colin, if you please. There's a wee matter here to be discussed."

While the crewmen opened the hatches and began stowing the catch, Colin Campbell jumped aboard, and clambered forward to the fo'c'sle.

Angus John sat at the mess table in the cramped quarters of himself and the crew, a steaming mug clasped in his hands. The glistening oilskins and creaking boots of Colin Campbell, short of stature but built like an Ayrshire bull, filled the hatchway as he descended the ladder.

"There's tea on the stove," Angus John greeted him without looking up.

Colin eased himself behind the table opposite his partner and stirred the tea in silence.

"We'll have to dump them, I suppose," Angus John said, scratching his chin and glancing up at his companion.

"It would be the proper thing to do," agreed Colin, avoiding the other's eyes.

"Och, no doubt about that," concurred Angus John, "the proper thing indeed. But, there would be no great harm in keeping just one or two for the pot . . . eh, Colin?"

Ashore, in the little graveyard by the harbour, past generations of respectable Campbells stirred uneasily in their eternal sleep as Colin sipped at his mug and considered the suggestion.

"No—no real harm, I would think," he judged. "Just a meal or two for the lads. Aye, and maybe even a small one for the widow McDougall and her with no man to provide since Iain, God rest him, passed away."

"It would certainly be of Christian charity," acclaimed Angus John, refilling his mug at the stove. Then, as if a sudden thought had occured to him. "A few pounds extra in her purse, with Christmas not that far off, would be a greater kindness don't you think, Colin?"

"Man, but you're right there." Colin had a fine regard for the giving and receiving at Christmas. "Ach, but it's a great shame that's in it," he sighed. "Once in a lifetime you have such luck and nothing to be done but turn your back on it. A shameful waste."

"A truer word you've never spoken," Angus John was on his feet looking down at his partner with the solemnity of a minister on a Sabbath morning. "Waste is a mortal sin. It says so in the Good Book. Are the lads to go home with empty pockets after a hard night when Himself in His goodness has filled the hold with His bounty?"

The full implication of Angus John's words registered with Colin as he licked his lips, suddenly turned dry. "But the law, Angus," he managed, hoarsely.

"The law," Angus John laughed. "What do lawyers know about our life? If they spent just one night at the nets with us, and a family to clothe and feed, their havers might be worth listening to. The fish were put in the sea to be caught by the likes of you and me, Colin old friend, and no *bodach* in a fancy wig is going to tell us what we may or may not take." Angus John's chest was heaving as his smouldering eyes sought those of his partner. "Well, Colin, are you with me?"

In the little graveyard by the harbour, the generations of worthy Campbells awaited their descendent's reply with considerable agitation. That is with one exception, Andrew Campbell, who died in mysterious circumstances, his pocket filled with golden sovereigns. But then, having had a McGregor for a mother, he doubtless viewed Colin's dilemma with a greater degree of understanding than his fellows.

"My hand on it, Angus," boomed Colin, surging to his feet, his partner's fingers crushed in his ox-like grip.

Like boys released from school, the two abandoned the

fo'c'sle, crossed the swaying deck and stared down at their catch in the hold—a fortune to them in sterling silver salmon.

"*Mo creach*," gasped Colin, "near on two thousand pounds hard cash, or I'm no judge."

"Aye, there is that," replied Angus John, his mind already grappling with the pressing problem of disposal.

"A mite difficult to get rid of, though," pointed out Colin, rubbing his forehead.

"I've been giving that some thought," replied Angus John. "Lachie Begg will be at the sale in the morning, for a scatter of herring for his wee bit of a kipper-house, wouldn't you say?"

"Nothing surer," confirmed Colin, "a dozen or so baskets as cheap as he can get them. *Bho, bho,* but its the tight one is Lachie, even if he is your own cousin, Angus."

"Myself knows that well enough. Don't you see, Colin, a better man for our bit business we couldn't hope to find. I'll see Lachie before the sale and tell him that we've just a few baskets of the best herring ever and that, as his cousin, I'd be heart sick at the thought of the others getting the better of him. I'll tell him that he'll be able to double the price of his kippers and as blood is thicker than water, I'll box them myself and deliver them to his yard at no extra cost."

"*Och nan och*, with the meanness that's in the man he'll bid over the odds, if he has to, in expectation of making the grand profit." Colin's enthusiasm knew no bounds. "None of the big buyers will be interested in so few baskets anyway."

"Once we have the boxes in his shed, a phone call to a friend . . . er . . . a man I met once in FWilliam, and they will be away to Glasgow before the day's out," advised Angus John.

"But, what about Lachie when he finds not a tail of a

herring to be found in his shed?" Colin had a point.

"No problem," Angus John winked craftily, "he'll not be at the kippering till the evening, and before then I'll tell him that the herring were a bitter disappointment when I saw them in the boxes. I'll say, with the rage that was on me, I threw them over the quay, but that my conscience would be troubled if he refused to accept full payment for his loss.

"I'm not thinking you'll have any difficulty persuading him to take your money," chuckled Colin, slapping his massive thighs. "*A dhia, tha thu cho ligheach ri sionnach.*" To have his cunning equated with that of a fox, the skipper of the Eriskay Lass considered a mark of the highest esteem.

The first grey tinge of dawn edged the hills behind the harbour as the boats of the herring fleet tied up at the quay. Ropes secured, the fishermen, in ones and twos, trudged off up the pier to their homes to snatch a couple of hours sleep before the sales would begin.

In the cab of his lorry parked opposite the boats, Alec Crichton, herring-buyer, stretched and yawned. Although he had driven all day from his base at Aberdeen to be at the sales, he had been content to doze in the confines of the cab rather then spend "guid sillar" on a night's lodgings. "Bed's a' richt for sick folks and rich yeens but I'm neither," was his maxim.

He watched the men head homewards then, satisfied that he was alone on the pier, he opened the cab door and dropped lightly to the ground. A wee check of the quality of the herring in the holds before the auction would give him the edge on the other buyers, for he had little faith in the sample which the fishermen would put up for display at the sale. He crossed from boat to boat, lifting a hatch board and shining his torch into the hold, his experienced eye passing judgement on each catch. On reaching the Eriskay Lass however, instead of the mess of glistening herring, his beam illuminated a dozen fishboxes neatly stacked with the lids securely nailed down. This was not the way that herring were sold in the market, so if not herring in those boxes, then what?

A couple more boards removed and he was down into the hold. Using a metal scoop, which he found at his feet, he prised up the topmost lid. By the light of the torch he counted six, seven, eight fresh salmon, and not one under ten pounds in weight.

"Man Alec," he smiled to himself, "is yon no a sicht tae gladden the heart."

When the pale dawn had given way to a bright morning, buyers, lorry drivers and fishermen mingled on the pier, hands dug deep in pockets, cigarettes glowing, as they all waited for the catches to be auctioned. Baskets, each containing a scooped sample of herring and a ticket to identify the boat, were lined beside the salesman's rostrum. The last basket bore the legend, Eriskay Lass and the herring, hand picked from the best of the other boats by Colin, while Angus John distracted the owners in conversation, was by far the best and brightest on display.

The ringing of the auction bell brought all those interested before the salesman. The first basket was tipped across the sample board and the bidding began. The samples progressed until finally that of the Eriskay Lass was exposed.

"Well gentlemen, there you see them, just a dozen baskets, but of good quality," the salesman announced. "Who'll start me at seven pounds?"

The herring were certainly of outstanding quality, but a mere dozen baskets, as Colin had foreseen, aroused no great interest among the big buyers with lorries and trailers to fill. The bidding began briskly enough, with Lachie Begg, fresh from his cousin's briefing and encouraged by nods from the latter from the far side of the gathering, among the leading contenders. The other buyers quickly fell out and when the salesman called, "Ten pounds once, ten pounds twice," the bid was with Lachie.

"And fifty pence." From the back of the crowd, Alec Crichton's voice came loud and clear.

"Ten and fifty at the back, do I hear eleven?" the salesman returned to the fray looking hopefully at Lachie. Glancing hurriedly behind to identify his opposition, he nodded his head. Like a tennis ball, the bidding went from Lachie's court to Alec Crichton's in leaps of fifty pence. In a state of rising panic, Angus John stared at his cousin, willing him to continue. At fourteen pounds, Lachie's true nature overcame the tenuous bonds of family loyalty and shaking his head, he retired from the contest.

With that, the sales were over for the day. Buyers and drivers moved off to manoeuvre the lorries to the berths for the loading. Angus John stood rock-still in their midst, stunned by the turn of events.

"A've backed the larrie up tae yon space at the edge o' the pier, so, if ye bring yer boatie roun' yer laddies can load the boxes on the tail, they'll just mak up the load fine."

Snapping out of his stupor, Angus John looked down at the little Aberdonian in faded overalls standing before him. Why, he asked himself, had this wee man paid such a high price for a dozen baskets of herring, when he could have easily filled his lorry a great deal cheaper from the other boats. And how did he know that they were already boxed—a job normally done by the buyer himself so that he can check the quality as the fish are winched out of the hold?

"You'll be wanting to see them before we load, no doubt," said Angus John, forcing a smile, his eyes riveted on those of the buyer. "I'll get one of the lads to open the lids for you."

"Na, na, dinna bother. Ye hae an honest face freend and besides, I'm in a terrible hurry. Just load them on the larry while I'm awa settling the account wi the salesman. A'll be watchin frae his office window. If ye need me, jist gie a wave."

Angus John knew that no buyer in his right mind would accept herring from a boat without checking them against the sale-sample and this man, he reckoned, was no fool. Somehow Alec Crichton must have known, that the herring he was bidding for were worth their weight in gold. He returned to the boat and gestured across the gunwale to his partner.

"A word with you Colin, for'ard if you please."

"What's to be done, Angus? We'll be in jail this day, every mother's son of us," Colin Campbell prophesied, disgrace staring him in the face. "*Mo creach*, why did I ever let you talk me into this?"

"Wheest man," Angus John snapped. "That wee *bodach* knows fine well what he's bought, so he'll not be running to the police, that's for sure." It was not so much the loss of money that rankled but to be bested by an Eastcoaster on his own pier that he'd never live down. "Tell the lads to bring the boat round and to load the boxes on the lorry—but let them take their time about it. I'll be back shortly."

Angus John slipped ashore and made his way, as he had always done since a boy when in trouble, to a whitewashed cottage at the head of the pier, the home of his grandmother, Katie McLellan.

"It's yourself, Mrs McLellan," Constable Calum McKinnon welcomed the grey-haired woman on the doorstep of the Police Office some time later. "Come you through and have a seat. I'm not seeing much of you these days."

The visitor comfortably seated on his own chair at the

desk, Calum allowed her to come to the reason for her visit in her own good time. Without being too precise as to the identity of the principals and alluding to the merchandise in question as "the strange ones"—the word salmon being considered the worst possible luck on the lips of fisher-folk—the situation at the pier gradually unfolded.

"To be found in possession of a certain kind of "fish" could have unfortunate consequences at law, you'll understand, Mrs McLellan," advised Calum in the detached manner of a solicitor propounding on a hypothetical case in which he was not himself involved.

The old lady sat stiffly, hands clasped in her lap, nodding her head at the rightness of Calum's pronouncement. If he had not made such a declaration at the outset, she'd have been disappointed, for she had the greatest respect for the principle of law and order. The official view thus stated, she awaited Calum's own solution to the problem.

"However," he resumed, "there's not only the letter, but also the spirit of the law to be considered."

"Indeed there's that, Constable McKinnon," she readily concurred.

"If the profits from such a venture were to line the pockets of unscrupulous men," reasoned Calum, "then the law should be, and rightly so, unmerciful." The grey head nodded vigorously in agreement. "But, if the articles in question were acquired incidentally while the recipients were plying their lawful trade and if the proceeds were to be used for the general benefit of a community . . . say a new floor for the village hall or much needed slates for the church roof . . . then I'm thinking that the resulting good would outweigh any technical infringement which may have inadvertantly been committed."

In Granny McLellan's opinion, Solomon in his wisdom

could not have interpreted the law more sensibly. But then, she had expected nothing less.

Calum next removed a somewhat dusty file from a shelf and carefully studied a routine report, which he had received weeks previously. The information contained seemed to give him food for thought. Replacing the file, he turned to gaze through the window at the harbour and, as though oblivious of his visitor's presence, he theorised aloud a course of action which, taken in conjunction with the report he'd just read, promised fair hope of a near mutually satisfactory resolution of a problem about which he was, of course, officially unaware.

Attentively, Granny McLellan eavesdropped Calum's deliberations then hurriedly taking her leave, departed the office back to her cottage where Angus John awaited her with mounting impatience. Within minutes he was again at the boat, Old Katie's instructions clear in his mind.

Checking that all twelve boxes had been loaded on the lorry, Alec Crichton parked near the head of the pier, drew the tarpaulin over the load and began securing the ropes.

Two seasoned crewmen from the Eriskay Lass, Thomas and Seamas, acting on the skipper's orders, wandered in the buyer's direction to pause, by chance, opposite his lorry. And well within earshot, as he tightened and knotted the ropes, struck up a casual conversation.

"The worst of luck ever, the poor souls," said Thomas, his eyes raised heavenwards in mild rebuke. "Who would have expected the Fishery Cruiser in the Minch last night?"

"A pure misfortune," harmonised Seamus. "They say they had the binoculars on them when they pulled the net and saw the salmon go aboard, clear as the nose on your face. It's a wonder the police weren't on the pier to nab them when they came in this morning."

"Och, you're not understanding these things, Seamus," scorned his companion. "It's the one who buys the fish they want to catch. A resetter, they call him. Man, but it's the desperate serious view the courts take of resetters."

As the two moved off, Alec Crichton scrambled into the cab of his lorry. The engine sprang to life and he was away, long-hauling it on the road to Fort William. He reckoned that by the time the country bobbies got themselves organised, he'd be half-way to Aberdeen.

Humming to himself, he throttled down round a twisting bend then, as the road opened before him, his foot rammed down hard on the brake pedal. Less then a hundred yards ahead, a uniformed Constable McKinnon was pulling back the tarpaulin of a stationary lorry. A farm entrance offered a turning-place. Crashing his gears in his haste, he headed back the way he had come.

Seated on an upturned fish-box, Colin Campbell, patiently whittling a piece of wood, pocketed his knife and sauntered across to where Alec Crichton's vehicle had come to a stop. "You didn't get far, Colin remarked with concern. "Nothing wrong, I hope?"

"Naething serious like," the buyer answered, glancing back the way nervously. "A bit trouble wae the fuel injection, ye ken. I can cure it in twa minutes."

"Och, there's no need to hurry, you're not likely to get far this day."

"Whit d'ye mean by that?" The fisherman's words had sounded like the clang of a cell door in Alec Crichton's ears.

"It's just that the postmen was saying, that you can't move for policemen on the Fort William road. They're stopping and searcing every lorry. *A dhia*, they're nothing if not thorough, those boys."

"Whit . . . eh . . . are the seekin like?" asked the buyer running a finger inside his collar.

"I've no idea," Colin shrugged his expansive shoulders. But, whatever it is, they'll find it."

Alec Crichton chewed on his lip. It was only a matter of time before the police reached the village and he was trapped. There was no other way out of the accursed place.

"It reminds me just of a winter we had a few years back." Colin was in a conversational mood. "We were completely snowed in, nothing getting through at all."

"Aye, that would be richt awkward," murmured the buyer with problems enough of his own to worry about.

"Awkward was hardly the word for it. No bread or milk, nothing for three days. If it hadn't been for the fishing boats bringing stores from Oban, I don't know what would have happened to us."

Colin let this piece of information sink in, then he added. "The only way in—and out—was by boat."

"By boat, ye say?" Alec Crichton grasped at the word like a drowning man. "Listen freen, I hae a dozen boxes o' prime herrin' that I must get tae Aberdeen afore the mornin— a vera special customer, ye ken. Wi a' this polis nonsense I'll never mak it. Dae ye think yin o' yon boats micht be persuaded tae tak them tae Oban and put them on the train for me, richt noo like?" A'd nae stint at the payin' ye ken."

Colin stroked his chin and creased his brows as he considered the buyer's query.

"Well," he replied hesitantly, "this being Friday, there'll be no boats going out to the fishing tonight. It might be that I could find someone who'd run the herring for you if the price was right, of course."

"Hae nae fear on that account. A'd see him a' richt."

Colin moved off to mingle with a group of fishermen, then he returned all smiles to the fidgeting Alec Crichton.

"Though I say it myself, it wasn't easy," he declared. "But put your mind at ease. I''ve found one decent man who won't see you stuck. Just you back the lorry to the edge of the pier and he'll be along in no time.

Alec Crichton swung lightly into the cab and reversed to the appointed spot. Colin followed, opened the passenger door and heaved himself into the seat. In the mirror he could discern the Eriskay Lass nose up to the pier behind him.

"You were talking about payment," Colin mentioned in a manner that suggested that the matter was of only passing interest to him.

"Ah did that," confirmed the buyer, pulling out his cheque book. "Noo freen, whit would you ca' a reasonable price?"

The skipper was thinking that, maybe sixty pounds would not be too much—"to cover the oil, and a wee something for the crew, you'll understand."

"Vera reasonable indeed," accepted the buyer, trying not to show his delight at the bargain. Opening the cheque book across his knee, he unscrewed the top from his pen.

At that very moment, the squeal of protesting tyres caused both men to look up. A police patrol car sped through the village coming shuddering to a halt at one of the lorries ahead of them. Constable Calum McKinnon got out of the car and strode purposefully to the parked vehicle. They watched as he jerked open the cab door. Seconds later, accompanied by the driver, he marched to the rear of the lorry and began untying the ropes of the hap which covered the load.

With trembling fingers, Alec Crichton leaned forward to begin writing. Colin's ham-sized hand stayed him. "There is of course the question of insurance to be considered," he said.

"Insurance?"

"Aye, just that," Colin confirmed. "The skipper was thinking that two thousand would about cover it."

"Twa thousand pound insurance, for a dozen boxes o' herrin', are ye oot o' yer senses, man?" Alec Crichton exploded, outrage overcoming his fear.

"Ah, but these are rather special herring, are they not," suggested Colin, craning his head forward for a better view of Calum's activities. "I see that the policeman has finished with that lorry and started on the one in front of us. You'll be next, no doubt." He reached for the handle of the door. "I'd better be leaving you now. I wouldn't like that policeman thinking that we're in business together if you follow my meaning."

The buyer's eyes switched to the lorry in front. Calum's black uniform and diced cap came sharply into focus. "Twa thousand, ye said," he surrendered, and started to write.

"And sixty for the oil, if you remember," corrected Colin, amiably. "You can make the cheque out to, Mrs Katie McLellan. She's the grandmother of Angus John, the man you bought the . . . er . . . herrings from, so you'll know him fine."

"Aye, I ken him," hissed the buyer, tearing out the cheque and thrusting it at Colin.

After examining it carefully, the skipper wound down the window and sticking his head out he shouted, "You can start with the unloading, lads. As quick as possible. The gentleman is in something of a hurry." Turning to the shrunken figure of the buyer, he took his leave. "Rest assured, the boxes will be on the train for Aberdeen—cash on delivery, of course."

Seconds after Alec Crichton heard the last box dragged from the tail of his lorry, the cab door was pulled open and

Constable McKinnon appeared before him.

"Acting on information received," Calum intoned, "I have reason to suspect that you may be in breach of the law by what you have on this lorry. I intend to make a search of this vehicle and . . ."

"Search awa' Constable," interrupted the buyer, the engine noise of the Eriskay Lass sweet music to his ears as she drew away from the quay. "A've naethin' but herrin'. Whit else would ye expect to find . . . bars o' gold like?"

"No, sir," replied Calum, "a dog, small, possibly a terrier."

"A dug?" the relevence of dogs to the situation escaped the buyer.

"Yes sir, a dog. It is my information that a lorry was observed to accept such an animal from a foreign yacht. This would consitute an offence under Orders relating to the importation of dogs, cats and other mammals. A very serious crime indeed, sir."

"Ye mean a' this stoppin' and searchin' o' larries has been o'er naething mair than a dug . . . naething else?"

"I don't think you appreciate the gravity of the matter," admonished Calum.

"The gravity o' the matter?" Alec Crichton wheezed, the fierceness of his grasp on the steering-wheel causing his knuckles to show white. "A hae twa thousand guid reasons for kennin' the gravity o' the matter."

In the wheel-house of the Eriskay Lass, as she cleared the shelter of the harbour, her bow biting into a choppy sea, Angus John, his legs braced against the rise and fall of the deck, spun the spokes through his fingers and set course for Oban.

"Och nan och, Colin, but yon was a near thing," he

confessed to his partner, then he chuckled. "That ploy of Old Katie's about the contraband dog was just sublime. *A dhia*, it's the fly old head that she has on her shoulders, to be sure."

"She has that," conceeded Colin, "though it's a pity we never made a penny out of it for ourselves. Myself was having the thought, Angus, that, maybe next week . . ."

In the little churchyard by the harbour, Colin Campbell's saintly ancestors resumed their eternal rest, easy in the knowledge that their ancient name had remained unsullied. The exception was he of the golden sovereigns whose sleep was disturbed by the thought that one of his blood should emerge with empty pockets from so promising a venture.

Calum knocked his pipe out against the bole of the tree, and looked towards the river. "The sun's off the water now, Roddy. I'm thinking we could try a cast or two."

"It's maybe as well they never got round to promoting you, Calum," the Minister grinned, rising and picking up his rod. "If left to you, the jails would all be empty."

4

I Left it to Calum

Seated at a cluttered desk in his island Police Office, Constable Calum McKinnon signed, dated and filed a report on a teenager who, having been declared missing from the mainland, had been found that morning on Beinn Mhor, soaked to the skin and down to his last tin of beans. Fetched off the island by his parents on the afternoon ferry, he had departed openly defiant but inwardly relieved.

Idly, Calum flicked back through past Missing Persons reports, some of which would stay perhaps for ever incomplete. He paused at one such and there was anger mellowed by sadness in his eyes as he scanned the typewritten sheet. It referred to a local fisherman, lost at sea a number of years past, when his boat had gone down with all hands. His body had not been recovered. The file had been closed, marked Presumed Dead and would no doubt remain so.

At the sound of the office door closing, he looked up to find a young man with a haversack on his back, standing at the counter.

"I wonder, Constable," the arrival asked, " if you could give me some information. It's about the sinking of a fishing-boat called the Eilidh. From the memorial in the cemetery, I understand that one of the crew was never found."

"Man, but is that not the strange thing," replied Calum, rising to his feet with the file in his hand. "That's the very report I've just been reading, and it gathering dust these past ten years." Placing the file on the counter he read aloud to the young man the relevant passages . . . time, place and probable cause of the sinking, names, dates of birth and addresses of the deceased. "A sad business," Calum deplored, returning the file to its shelf. "They're sorely missed, to be sure."

The young man made no move to leave and Calum sensed that there was still something he wanted to say or ask, yet was unsure how to begin. To give him time to order his thoughts, Calum bemoaned, at some length, the poor weather they'd had on the island that year. Then remarking on his visitor's fine sun-tan, he wondered if he'd been abroad. This seemed to give the young man the opening he'd been seeking.

With a view to improving his fluency in the language and to widen his horizons, Calum learned that the student, for such was his visitor, had spent the long vacation from university hitch hiking through Germany, arriving at length in the mountain regions of Bavaria.

"With limited funds," the student continued, "I travelled, for the most part on foot. In need of a rest, I checked my map and decided to stop for a few days at a village which, I noted, lay slightly off the main tourist route.

"I had no difficulty in finding lodgings at reasonable cost and after a good soak in a warm bath, I set out to explore the place. The wide-gabled, wooden-balconied houses were a delight to see and I took a special pleasure in the old world paintings which by tradition decorate the otherwise white facades of the buildings.

"As the day wore on, I found the heat oppressive, so it was a relief to sit down at a table of a pavement cafe and indulge myself by ordering a long, cool ice-drink. As I waited for it to arrive, my attention was drawn to the house directly opposite. On a ladder placed against the wall, a man was re-touching the colours, faded by sun and weather, of a larger-than-life representation of a bent old man in peasant dress, staff in hand, lantern held high. I sipped my drink and with mounting interest, watched the waning colours revive and bloom again beneath the brush.

"I had been observing him for quite a time, when he descended and took several steps backwards, bringing him close to my table. Hands on hips, he examined his work then shook his head with evident dissatisfaction. This surprised me, for I could see no flaw in the workmanship.

"It's very good," I commended, in my best German. "Really excellent." It seemed for a time that either he hadn't understood or had chosen to ignore me. I was about to rise and leave when, wiping his hands on a piece of rag, and without turning his head, he said.

"It's generous of you to say so, young friend, but I'm afraid I can't agree with you."

"Startled, I stared at him, for he had spoken not with the slow Bavarian drawl which I would have expected, but in the lilting English of the Gael.

"Myself will have to be doing his coat again. It's a shade too dark for my liking," he judged, turning in my direction. Two penetrating blue eyes surveyed me from a weathered face, the bristles of several days' growth on his chin, ginger coloured in the sunlight. "The old fellow's been up there more years than you or I have seen, so I'm not thinking that another day or two will make much difference to him." As he made to move off, I felt impelled to detain him and invited him to join me for a refreshment, indicating an empty chair at my table.

"Well now," he hesitated, his eyes thoughtful as he looked down at me, as though assessing my suitability as a drinking companion. "I've never been known to refuse a dram."

He settled himself opposite me but, as I was about to signal for service, the waitress, her round, beaming face framed by braids of blond hair, placed a brimming glass before him. At some aside which he made to her, she bubbled with laughter and flounced off in mock indignation. My guest saluted me with the glass and drained it at a gulp.

"You must be a regular here," I smiled, nodding in the direction of the waitress.

"Aye, you could say that," he conceded.

"My name's Anderson . . . Ian Anderson. I'm from Glasgow," I introduced myself. And you, unless my ears deceive me, are from further North, one of the islands, perhaps?"

"A fair enough city, Glasgow, so I've heard tell," he answered noncommittally, indicating to the waitress the emptiness of his glass. "You'll be on holiday, no doubt," he suggested, leaning back and eyeing my hiking boots and shorts.

"As I lay in bed that night, I realised with some annoyance, that although we had spent the best part of two hours together and I had related my entire history from cot to college I had learned almost nothing about the painter.

"At breakfast the following morning, I learned from my landlady, that the painter had arrived in the village 3 or 4 years previously possessing little more than a few brushes and tubes of paint. While his money lasted, he had lodged at the very house in which I was staying and had done a number of paintings of the the locality, a few of which he had been able to sell to the tourists. Unfortunately, sales had not proved equal to his needs and rent payments had fallen hopelessly in arrears. My landlady had accepted the odd picture in exchange for board, but finally economics had dictated that they should part. However, his ability with the brush had not gone unnoticed and he now earned a living by re-touching and creating new wall paintings, without which the village would lose much of its attraction.

"As to his identity, my landlady had to confess that, in common with the rest of the villagers, she knew him only as Schottie, a name they had given him on account of his nationality and which he seemed happy to accept.

"That afternoon I returned to my table at the cafe and as on the previous day, Schottie abandoned his work in the heat of the sun and joined me, as if by appointment. What had begun as a chance encounter became for both of us, I flatter myself to think, an agreeable daily routine. He talked knowledgeably of the Renaissance masters and of his own contemporaries, graphically of his life in Paris and ruefully of attic studios quitted by moonlight for the lack of a few coins to pay the rent. I learned early in out relationship to curb my natural curiosity concerning his origins. Nevertheless, whenever I alluded to our common homeland or to some aspect of Scottish life, I sensed his immediate if suppressed interest.

"The expectation of spending my whole vacation abroad was dispelled when I checked my finances after less than a week's stay in the village. My artist friend had an infinite capacity for downing glasses without the fiery liquid, as far as I could see, having an effect on him other than sharpening his appetite for the richly garnished steaks, provided by the cafe and paid for invariably by myself. My acquaintance with Schottie had all but beggared me.

"The day prior to my departure, I went as usual to the cafe with the intention of taking my leave of Schottie but found, to my disappointment, no trace of him. After waiting considerably beyond our normal time of meeting, I called the waitress and asked if she had seen anything of him that day. I was surprised to see that, at the mention of his name, her usual gaiety deserted her. She told me that he had spent the whole morning at the cafe, his glass in regular need of refilling. She had coaxed him to stop but had finally refused him further service.

"Schottie is a kind, good man," she told me, defensively. Then with just a hint of accusation, "Meeting you has made him homesick, I think."

"Where can I find him?" I asked her with concern.

"He has a room above the baker's shop, there," she pointed down the street.

"I found the shop and climbed the stairs leading to the upper floor. Receiving no reply to my repeated knocking, I tried the handle and finding the door unlocked, I entered.

"The room boasted only the minimum of furnishings. Below the wide attic window stood an easel supporting a partially finished landscape canvass. At a bare kitchen table sat Schottie, unshaven, unkempt, his half-shut eyes staring through a straggle of red hair across his face, a glass clasped before him.

"It was late evening before I left him and returned to my lodgings. With me I carried away a small parting gift which he had seen fit to give me. I took away also a garbled account of his early life, which I had gleaned from his ravings, before getting him safely to bed.

"I arrived back in Scotland with just enough money for the return fare to this island. My first priority was a visit to the cemetery. I searched among the headstones till I found what I was looking for . . . a memorial to four fishermen, drowned when their boat the Eilidh sank in the winter of '69. Three lay at rest among their kin, but the fourth, Roderick McPherson, was remembered in name only. The sea had, it seems, kept him for herself. From the graveyard, I headed for your office."

Calum had listened to the student's recital of his wanderings, to begin with out of politeness, then, when the young man described his chance meeting with the painter in far off Bavaria, with the closest attention.

In the circumstances, Calum felt obliged to offer his visitor, from his own personal knowledge, a fuller account than the police report could supply, of the man in whose fate they both undoubtedly shared a common concern.

"A sickly child," Calum began. "Born to a family of hardy fisherfolk, Roderick McPherson . . . or Roddy as he was known . . . had been dominated by a mother determined against all the evidence of Nature to make a man of him. He grew to adulthood, cowed and totally subservient to her will.

"A mutual interest in drawing and painting was a sort of bond between me and Roddy. Och, but it's the rare talent that he had," Calum declared, his admiration genuine. "I was just a dabbler compared with him. At home he could do nothing right. But put him before a canvass, with a brush in his hand, and man, he was in his real element. He could have been a great artist if only his mother . . . and that wildcat of a wife she got him . . . had had the gumption to see it."

"He was married, then?" the student asked, innoccently.

"*A dhia* yes," Calum confirmed. "No man more so. It was not long after his father died that his mother arranged it, as she did everything else in his life. Kate Mungo, as she was called then, has a tongue at her that sharp that no man in his right senses would willingly go within a mile of her.

"Well, if poor Roddy's life was a misery before he wed, it was pure Hell afterwards, with the two of them hounding him from dawn to dusk. He hated the fishing, but to the fishing he had to go . . . they made sure of that. God forgive me, but those two witches of women sent him to his death, as sure as I'm standing here." The anger in Calum's voice was undisguised.

"It would be hard for them afterwards . . . two women alone, I mean," the student ventured.

"Don't you believe it," Calum scoffed. "Never were they better off than when they lost Roddy."

"I don't follow . . ."

"The insurance money," Calum exploded. "Man, but it's the pretty penny they got from the insurance on his life. They bought a big house, a mile up the road, and started taking in boarders. A real gold mine it is with the tourists and all. Ach, but it makes me sick to think of those two women, and that poor fool, Hughie Martin . . . Kate married him a couple of years after the sinking . . . lording it in that fine house and not a thought for Roddy and him worth the lot of them put together."

"And they never did find McPherson's body, did they?" the student made the question sound casual.

"No, never," Calum agreed, bitterly.

"I read once," the student said, "of a boat that sank with all hands lost and, like the Eilidh, one man not accounted for. There was quite a stir when he turned up, years later, in Australia. Apparently, the night before they sailed, he slipped ashore for, like Roderick McPherson, he had no heart for the seafaring. When the boat sank and the bodies were recovered the following morning, it was assumed that he had gone down with her. As he had no one at home who cared whether he lived or died, he decided to stay missing and seek a new life. Did well for himself out there, by all accounts."

"Well, if his life was anything like Roddy's, I'd not be blaming him if he did a runner, as they say," condoned Calum.

"I'd be grateful, Constable," the student said, withdrawing from his haversack a rectangular shaped package, "as a man with an interest in painting, if you would care to give me your opinion of this one? It was given to me by the artist himself, when I was in Germany."

Calum stripped off the brown paper covering, and examined the painting, at arm's length, then closely and in detail.

Observing the changing expressions on the Constable's face as he studied the picture, the student recalled the Schottie's words on that last evening together—"Here lad, you can have this one, I've plenty more. It's not big and will fit fine in your haversack. Hold on . . . I'll sign and date it."

Slowly Calum lowered the canvas and, in the silence of the room, their eyes met, and held.

"I've just had a thought, Constable," the student said, retrieving the painting from Calum's unresisting hands and wrapping it again in the paper. "I'd rather like Roddy's mother and widow to have this painting. A small reminder of a loving one now departed, though perhaps not quite so . . . irrevocably departed . . . as that memorial in the cemetery would suggest."

"You'll be wanting to catch the next ferry back, I'm thinking," Calum advised rather than enquired.

"That had been my intention," the student acknowledged as they both glanced at the office clock.

"Then there won't be time for you to deliver this in person," Calum said, his fingers lightly tapping the package on the counter.

"Not if I'm to catch that boat," the student agreed. "And it could get damaged in the post," he added.

"Indeed, you have the right of it there," Calum confirmed with equal concern. Then, as the obvious solution to the problem occurred to him, he suggested, "I'll be passing their house later today, and could deliver it for you if you like."

"That would be grand," the student enthused. "If you're sure it wouldn't be too much trouble?"

"Trouble?" a mirthless smile broadening his face, his large hands reverently smoothing the brown paper package. "Och, dear me no, no trouble at all, believe you me."

The student picked up his haversack and turned towards the door.

"I wonder," Calum said, "we often get foreign artists coming here to paint. Would you be thinking that perhaps . . ."

With his hand on the door handle the student remembered the waitress's words when she directed him to the attic where Schottie lodged, "Meeting you has made him homesick."

"I wouldn't be surprised, Constable," he answered, opening the door and raising his arm in farewell. "I wouldn't be at all surprised."

5

Calum . . . the Confessor

It had been a number of years since Calum McKinnon had
seen his cousin, Willie. Raised on neighbouring crofts they
had been close as boys but when Calum had joined the police
force and Willie had gone to the mainland to work at the
forestry, their subsequent meetings had been confined mainly
to family weddings and funerals.

A favourable opportunity for a surprise visit to Willie
offered itself when, returning to Oban from an escort duty to
Glasgow, Calum 'inadvertently' forked left on to a minor road
near the village of Kilmelford in spite of the sign-posted
indications that his goal lay, uncompromisingly, northwards.
Happily, the long miles of the journey had so wearied the young
constable who accompanied him that Calum's navigational
error went completely unnoticed. It was the patrol car drawing

to a halt before an isolated cottage, close by the sea which roused the infant lawman.

"Where are we?" he reasonably inquired, rubbing the sleep from his eyes.

"Where indeed?" said Calum, glancing around with the wonder of an astronaut newly arrived on the moon. "I'm thinking that, maybe, we're a wee bit lost." Then, with just the hint of accusation in his tone, "If someone, not sitting a hundred miles from here, had done a bit less snoring and a little more, semper vigilo-ing, we'd be snug back in Oban by now."

The look of shamed embarrassment on the young man's face twinged Calum's conscience.

"Och, it's no great disaster. I'll just be asking directions at this house and if there's a cup o' tea going, I'll give you a shout."

Fully ten minutes passed before the constable was called in for the hoped-for cup of tea, for the news Calum had received from Willie's wife, hadn't been good. Hospitably, she settled the fledgling at the kitchen table, a steaming cup and plate of fresh buttered scones at his elbow, before leading Calum to the bedroom door.

"Go you through and see him," she invited. "He'll be no worse for a sight of yourself." And so it proved. The pale face on the pillow flushed with pleasure at the unexpected appearance of Calum. But a heroic attempt to sit up to greet his visitor failed dismally.

"*Gabh do Shocair,*" Calum admonished him to take it easy. "Just tell me, in you own good time what ails you, *a bhalaich.*"

Resigned, perhaps relieved, to be able at last to unburden his soul to the one person in the world he knew he could trust with a confidence, Cousin Willie sank back into the pillow and, step by step, recounted the events which had brought him to such a sorry pass.

It had all begun, it seemed, with Rob McColl's accident. Rob, who worked with Willie's squad, had been felling on the far slope of Beinn Gharbh when a rogue spruce had crashed down, several degrees off course, pinning him by the leg. By the time he had been released the limb had swollen badly, and he had been removed to the Cottage Hospital with a suspected fracture of the ankle. The squad knew that, painful as the injury must have been, it would be the loss of wages while off work which would really hurt, for a forest worker's earnings were not such that he could suffer the loss of a few pounds without it causing hardship.

The initial concern for Rob, however, waned somewhat, as the weeks passed into months with no sign of his returning to work. It was not that they envied him, warm between the blankets while they shivered their way to the hill at the break of day. Nor did they grudge the 50p regularly contributed from their wage packets to help him out. No, these things did not trouble them, for it was the very closeness of their forest society that ensured the individual's survival.

What did rankle, though, was that from time to time, while thinning near the marches of a private woodland, they would catch a glimpse of the invalid, between the trees, weilding his power-saw with an enthusiasm which he had never displayed while working with the squad. A degree of resentment was also felt by those who chanced to observe Rob's weekly arrival in the doctor's car park. With no apparent discomfort, he would vault from the driving seat of a newly acquired, up-to-date registered motor car of a decidedly sporty cut and take the entrance steps to the surgery in his stride two at a time. Once through the door, however, there would take place an immediate deterioration in his physical condition. Hands, pressed for support against both walls of the narrow passageway, he would hop on his 'good leg' the few remaining feet to the consulting room. Here he would collapse into a chair, utterly exhausted by the effort. The doctor, a humanitarian of middle years and failing eyesight, would unhesitatingly scribe for him a further certificate of unfitness for work, dispense a bottle of tonic and advise complete rest.

In the quiet of the evening by his fireside, his wife Kirsty, darning socks which were more darn than sock, Willie pondered the futility of his existence. Apply himself as he might, his saw could only clothe, feed and house him, and that, Willie concluded, was just not enough. He sought alternatives—an exercise which occupied him but briefly. For, with a wife to support and a tied house, there seemed to be none.

The sudden movement of Kirsty laying aside her mending, drew his attention. For perhaps an hour, she had been seated before him on a stool, bent over her work. Now, hands massaging the small of her back, she straightened to ease the stiffness in her frame, then rose to prepare their supper.

If inspiration comes to gifted men all of a sudden then Willie at that moment joined their ranks. Like a revelation, he perceived in the pained action of his wife's stretching, the alternative which had previously eluded him. As the appetising sizzle of frying sausages reached him from the cooker, the conviction grew in Willie's mind that, with a little nudge, the scales of fortune could be tipped in his favour.

"But where, precisely, does it hurt?" Dr McAdam asked, peering through the thick lenses of his spectacles at Willie's broad back, laid bare on the surgery couch.

"*A chiall*, Doctor, that would be hard to say," the patient replied weakly. "It could be almost anywhere if the notion was on it, and myself bent like an old *bodach* and the breath clean out of my body with the terrible twinges I could be having."

The frequent use of the conditional mood by his patients when describing their ailments, had puzzled the doctor, Lowland by birth and education, when he had first taken up a practice in the Highands. Although the custom often complicated his making an exact diagnosis, he had in time grown to accept it. He had assumed either a quite praiseworthy reluctance on the part of the natives to unduly bewail their lot, or as seemed more likely to him, an inability to accurately translate their outlandish Gaelic tongue into plain English.

"It might be that you've strained your back at work, possibly while lifting a log, for instance," the Doctor suggested, unconsciously adopting a degree of vagueness which would undoubtedly have won the approval of his clientele.

"That I could," agreed Willie.

"Well, you'd better rest it for a bit and we'll see how things are in a week's time," Dr McAdam instructed, reaching for his pad of sick certificates.

Close to a rocky cove and 3 miles of twisting single-track road from the village proper, stood Willie's cottage. Exposed in winter to the full fury of the Atlantic gales, it was of a summer's evening an idyllic spot. The western sky blazed red behind the black sweeps of the Mull mountains. The tireless waters of the ocean stirred the shingle shore.

Unlike his fellow sufferer, Rob McColl, Willie took his daily and not unrewarding exercise in the relative privacy of the shore line before his home. Early morning or late evening, dependng on the time of the low tides, he would clamber over the barnacled rocks, lifting and parting the glistening seaweed, harvesting the winkle crop. A summer visitor, ignorant of the preferred habitat of his little shelled cousins, might, in an hour or so, gather a potful for boiling before wearying of the pursuit. Willie, on the other hand, would have considered his day ill-spent if in the space of a tide he couldn't fill an eight-stone sack. At a market price of around £5 a stone and no deductions for the taxman, each winkle was money.

Medically speaking, there were few ailments more frustrating for the good Dr McAdam than sore backs, especially the "when the notion's on them" variety. When X-ray examination failed to show a cause and the patient appeared otherwise to be in robust health, the only other course left to him was to prescribe rest and let Nature perform her own miracle. As this treatment suited Willie admirably, his incapacity remained stable, week by week, with a slight improvement being admitted only when the possibility of hospitalisation was raised.

At their cottage, Kirsty was enraptured with her brand new electric cooker, and so protective of her brand new living-room suite, that Willie had to change out of his working clothes before being allowed to even approach it. Willie's 'sick money' bought the bread, but it was the winkles that spread the jam.

Daily, Willie transported his sack of winkles in the boot of his old car a dozen miles down the coast to the nearest town, where a bulk-buying merchant was happy to take all he could get on a strictly cash-in-hand, on-the-spot basis. This method of doing business was mutually beneficial to all the parties concerned, with but one exeption—that of the Department of Social Security. Like the Wicked Witch of the North it did not receive an invitation to attend, an omission which riled all the way to Head Office.

Having taken advantage of a mild Spring morning and a favourable tide, Willie was in high spirits as he motored the bends towards town. In the boot was an extra half-bag of prime winkles, a bonus for his early rise. Down the main street he drove, busy with shoppers, then left into Harbour Road at the far end of which the buyer's yard was situated.

Glancing in the rear view mirror, he was startled to observe a dark green coloured van about to overtake him at high speed. Willlie pulled to his near side and braked hard. The van scraped past, then shuddered to a halt across the yard entrance. Two men leaped from the vehicle almost before it had stopped, and disappeared through the gate at a run. Willie switched off the engine, his way to the yard blocked.

Moments later the men re-emerged flanking a dejected figure dressed in a stained raincoat and well-worn wellington boots. All three loaded into the van and with a triumphant roar of the engine they were off. The way now clear, Willie started up and continued on into the yard.

"*A dhia, a'bheil thu far do chinn?*" the buyer, displaying all the outward signs of cardiac arrest, advanced on Willie, demanding if he was out of his mind.

"*Bi samhach, a Dhomhnuill,*" Willie advised composure. "*De tha cearr?*" and asked what was wrong.

"Did you not see poor Seumas there and those two investigators from the 'Social' frog-marching the soul out like he was some desperate criminal. And now you here, bold as brass and yourself next on their list as like as not."

Willie was not the man to allow a modicum of risk to spoil his "wee bit business", as he termed it. So, with an indifferent shrug of the shoulders he dumped his sack on the scale. Oblivious of the buyer's impatience to be quit of him, Willie insisted on waiting till the pointer had quivered its last quiver and double checked the payment before thrusting it deep into his pocket. The deal completed, he felt it simple courtesy to pass the time of day with his benefactor before taking his leave.

"And how are herself's geraniums doing now, Donald? You were telling me that they were slow coming on the year." Willie had a fine memory for the things that mattered.

"Geraniums?" the buyer fumbled nervously with the yard keys. The sooner he could lock up and get safely home, the happier he would be. "Och, they're making nothing of it. She'll have to be dumping them, I'm thinking. I'll just check that the road's clear," he added pointedly, hurrying to the gate and looking anxiously in all directions.

"Aye, I'd better be on my way," Willie took the hint. I'll maybe mind to bring something for her plants that will do wonders for them next time I'm here."

The next day the weather continued mild. Willie was on the shore even before the sun was properly above the horizon. By mid-morning he was well ahead having filled one sack, which he left in a gully between two outcrops of rock, safely above water level. He was about to start on a second when, out of the corner of his eye, he saw the green-coloured van silently freewheel down the hill road, some distance behind him and turn off out of sight among the bushes at the entrance to a forestry track.

There was not the slightest doubt in Willie's mind that he had become the subject of "official observation".

A lesser man would prudently have taken to his heels across the rocks, but not Willie. There were rules, he knew, to the game of "hunt the winkler" and sportsman that he was, win or lose, he would play by them.

For an hour or so he worked away among the rocks by

the water's edge, keeping his back always to the road, but never out of sight. His movements were slow and laboured like those of an elderly gardener sore smitten with rheumatism, teasing weeds from his flower beds. Finally, hoisting the filled sack on his back, Willie stumbled up the shingle shore to his car parked by the roadside and heaved it into the boot.

For a vehicle of advanced years the car had a fair turn of speed and the green van, which he had spotted in the morror in hot pursuit, was a distance behind him and in some difficulty with the traffic in the main street when Willie turned into Harbour Road and eased to a halt in the buyer's yard.

"*Mo creach*, Willie, is it the jail you're after, coming in here this day and themselves maybe still about?" was the buyer's less then cordial welcome.

"Och, and it's the shame that should be on you, Donald, admonished Willie, withdrawing a crumpled £5 note from his pocket. "Is that a civilised way to be greeting a cash customer?"

The squeal of protesting tyres heralded the arrival of the green van through the yard gates. The occcupants, two clean cut, well nourished young men sprang out, positioning themselves with practised ease on either side of their quarry.

"I'll take that," the taller of the two purred, confiscating the £5 note out of Willie's hand. This is the evidence of the transaction completed."

"Now, what transation would that be?" Willie asked, mystified, glancing inquiringly from one to the other.

"Payment for the sack of winkles that we saw you gather this morning and which are now snug in the boot of your car here." The stranger emphasised his point by giving the lid a sharp rap with his knuckles.

"Winkles," said Willie with obvious disgust. "Och, I would not be advising anyone to be putting the likes in his mouth at all, at all . . . dirty, nasty things that they are. If it's the tasty meal you're after, gentlemen, I would recommend Donald here's salt herrings. Aye, with a new potato or two, and a glass of sour mild to be washing the lot down, you couldn't do better. And cheap too, though I say it myself."

A burst of cruel laughter exploded from the tall stranger. The pathetic attempts on the part of his captures to talk their way to freedom never failed to amuse him.

"Open the boot," he commanded.

Although several inches shorter than the stranger, Willie was not to be easily intimidated.

"And who might you be, to be giving me the orders?" he countered, looking his adversary square in the eye.

With a flourish, the man produced an official looking identity card. "Department of Social Security," he snapped. "Now, open up."

"I think you'd best do as they ask, Willie," the buyer urged. Regrettable as Willie's downfall might be to him, it was by far and away preferable to the possibility of police officers being summoned to his premises and poking their long noses into certain crates, temporarily stored in a corner of the yard, the presence of which he would be hard put to explain.

Deserted by his ally, out-numbered by the enemy, Willie struck his colours and raised the lid of the boot. Amid the litter of rusted tools and old oilskins nestled the offending sack—wet, and reeking decidedly of the deep.

"Fetch it out," the voice at his elbow directed.

Willie did as instructed, depositing the sack at their feet. Flicking open his pen-knife, the tall official cut the twine that secured the neck of the sack and thrust in his hand.

For the serious student of human behaviour there was, in the moments that followed, thesis material in the variety of facial expressions registered by the official. Gingerly he withdrew his arm and held aloft an oozing tangle of fetid plant life, plainly marine in origin.

"Chopped fine and mixed with peat, there's no better feeding for ailing plants than fresh cut seaweed," advised Willie, sagely. "Did I not promise to bring you something for your good lady's geraniums, the last time I was here, Donald?"

"You did, to be sure," confirmed the buyer, the gratitude in his voice occasioned, not so much by the medication for his wife's sickly plants, as the diminished prospect of a visit from the constabulary.

"Now, let me see, what was it that I came for?" Willie scratched his head to stimulate his memory. "Ach yes, that was it . . . I'll have a firkin of salt herring."

He turned to the officials, a saintly look of martyred innocence on his face. "With the scarceness of money, myself being on 'the sick', you'll understand, herring as cheap as I can get them will maybe see us through till better times."

Deftly Willie retrieved his £5 note from its erstwhile custodian and handed it over to the buyer as payment for his purchase. "I don't like to be imposing, and you the busy gentlemen that you are," said Willie, bravely but not too successfully disguising the agony he was experiencing as he bent to lift the quarter barrel of herring. "But with the way my back is . . . I'd be grateful for a bit of a hand getting this into the boot of my car."

The next day, Willie had himself the luxury of a long lie-in and a leisurely breakfast. Then, strolling along the road to the telephone kiosk, he dialled the buyer's number. The news was good. The investigators from the Department, who had been staying at a hotel in town, had paid their bill and departed, bag and baggage, doubtless to hunt less wary prey elsewhere. His pipe glowing satisfactorily, Willie set off towards the shore where the previous day's sack of winkles waited to be collected from the rock gully.

At the cottage, Kirsty was busy at the sink filling her bright, new, front-loading washing machine, when she heard the kitchen door open.

"You couldn't have timed it better, Willie," she called, above the sound of running water. "Come and show me again which of these buttons I should be pressing." Receiving no reply, she turned to see what was detaining her husband. Willie, bent like a half-shut knife, tottered forward, clutching at the table for support. "*A chiall,* you rascal," she scolded in mock anger, shaking the suds from her hands. "You can keep your play-acting for those who don't know you as well as I do. Come and help me this minute."

"Acting be dammed," Willie gasped, great beads of sweat standing on his brow. "I really have done for my back this time, lifting that sack off the shore. In the name of mercy woman, call the doctor."

Calum took his leave of Cousin Willie and, with his young companion agreeably stuffed with buttered scones beside him, he set course for Oban.

"The woman reckons that her man strained his back at work," informed the constable.

"There's not much danger of that happening to you," judged Calum, pressing down hard on the accelerator.

"I wouldn't be in the least surprised if he wasn't just swinging the lead. They're all at it these days," intoned the young man, wordly wise.

"Not so," replied Calum. "It's more a case of the lead swinging him, I'm thinking."

6
The Colonel

Constable Calum McKinnon stood at the head of the pier and watched the passengers disembark. The twice weekly arrival of the steamer were highlights in the otherwise even tempo of island life and all who had the time to spare would be there or there about.

With the summer at its height, tourists formed the greater part of the passengers with just the odd familiar face of a 'city islander' home for the holidays. He noted with some surprise how much Archie the Post's boy Colin had grown, back after his first term at university. "Aye Archie," he mused, "you've good cause to be proud there."

Suddenly, for Calum, the sun became less warm and the sky less blue. Striding from the gangway, he saw the imperious figure of Colonel Buller, late of The Guards and for the past few years Laird of Cill Chiarain Estate, the largest on the island.

The Colonel had never quite accepted the passing of the British Empire and he ruled his island realm with same belief in his own omnipotence as he had the kingdoms of the Rajahs in years gone by.

Calum glanced round desperately for some place of refuge—but too late.

"Ah, Constable McKinnon," hailed the Colonel, making his way towards Calum. "Been intending to have a word with you. Got some friends coming over for the fishing next week. Don't want any trouble like last year, eh . . . with that tinker fellow . . . what's his name . . . Williams, McWilliams or whatever? Blessed tent pitched slap-bang by the river and not so much as a by-your-leave. Confounded cheek!"

Alarm bells began to ring in Calum's head. Only last evening he had seen the tell-tale column of blue smoke rising beyond the woods by the river bank that announced the arrival of old Eachunn McWilliam and his wife Eilidh at their traditional summer camp site on the Colonel's estate.

"Well, sir, as a matter of fact . . ." began Calum, hoping to find some compromise which would allow the Colonel the enjoyment of his river and old McWilliam the usual spot for his tent.

"Had the same types in India," continued the Colonel, ignoring Calum's interruption as he would have done with a subaltern incautious eough to voice an opinion at the mess table. "Idle, shiftless lot. All take and no give. But by thunder, we knew how to handle them."

The almost silent arrival of a gleaming chauffeur-driven Daimler car forestalled Calum's further instruction on man management as practised in the colonies and baulked effectively any chance he had of settling the matter of the tinkers.

"Ah, MacFarlane at last," sounded the Colonel stepping into the car, the door held open by a deferential MacFarlane. With deliberation the Colonel extracted and studied the face of a gold pocket watch.

"Punctuality is not a virtue . . . it's a simple matter of self-discipline."

The admonition had been directed at MacFarlane but Calum had no doubt as he watched the car drive off, it had also been intended for his benefit.

Still, one had to respect the man. He had been all through the war—as he never tired of telling you. No doubt he had witnessed some terrible scenes and fought his way out of some tight corners. It couldn't have been easy for him to adjust to civvy life after an active military career. A good soldier, whatever his rank, is always respected in the islands.

The summons to the Big House came as Calum had expected, early the next morning. From the top step of the stairway leading to the oaked-door entrance to Cill Chiarain House, the Colonel wasted no time in greetings.

"Really McKinnon, I thought I'd made myself crystal clear yesterday about those tinkers."

"I tried to explain on the pier that . . ." Calum began.

"Dash it all, man, they're back where they were last year, slap on the river bank. A fire lit. Pots and rubbish everywhere. Expect they've been at the fish too. The pool's probably cleaned out! No principles these people, McKinnon. No respect for the other chaps' property."

Calum knew there would be no reasoning with the Colonel, but he had to try. He staightened his shoulders.

"Old Eachunn and his wife Eilidh have been coming to

this island for the potato lifting as long as anyone can remember. He's no thief and the pair of them work harder than a dozen men half their age."

"Nonsense, McKinnon. I know them. Had the same wallas in the war. No character, don't y'see? When the cards were down . . . ran like rabbits. Steal the water-bottle from a dying man without turning a hair. You're too soft McKinnon. Must show them who's in charge. Be a good chap now and see them off . . . double quick, or . . ."

The Colonel stopped, staring beyond Calum. His complexion changed from ruddy to florid. Turning his head, Calum followed the Colonel's line of vision. At the kitchen door of the house stood a tall slightly bent, bearded man wearing on his head a faded blue turban. It was Rangi Singh, the Indian pedlar, who came every year with his wares.

"D'you see McKinnon?" The Colonel's voice shook with anger.

"Let one in and before you can turn the place is swarming with them. Right. I'll handle this. Be a lesson to you."

Surging past Calum, the Colonel strode towards the pedlar with the authority of generations of colonels in his raised voice.

For some moments the pedlar suffered the Colonel, head bowed. Then, slowly, he raised his eyes. Soft and gentle brown his intent gaze met the Colonel's from a dark, grey-bearded face.

With some astonishment Calum heard the Colonel falter in mid-sentence. The colour drained from him. For what seemed like an eternity the two stared at each other in complete silence. Then slowly the Indian bent, picked up his suitcase and, with dignity, walked off down the drive.

Calum watched the departing figure for some moments.

When he turned it was to see the Colonel hurry inside and shut the door.

Calum invented all manner of reasons that day to delay his dutiful visit to old McWilliam's encampment to order him off. Finally, as the sun tipped the peak of Beinn Bhreac at the back of the village, he made his way to the site by the river.

As he approached, with the light just beginning to wane, he saw two figures seated by the embers of a wood fire close by the tent. The first he knew, by the shock of snow-white hair and the ever present cloud of lung-searing pipe smoke rising lazily in the still evening, to be old Eachunn McWilliam. The second was the turbaned Rangi Singh.

"*Feasgar math a Chaluim*," the old tinker greeted him. Calum returned the Gaelic welcome, then, out of consideration for the stranger, pursured the traditional analysis of the weather, present, past and to come, in English. After a little, old Eachunn motioned him to a seat on a log and drawing heavily on his pipe, turned to the business in hand.

"Himself of the Big House wil have sent you, I'm thinking."

"The same," replied Calum. "Himself, to be sure."

"Yourself will be acquainted with my friend, Rangi Singh?" queried the old man. "But perhaps you will not be knowing why he is ever welcome at my fire."

Calum acknowledged a passing acquaintance with the Indian. The old tinker continued.

"We had a son, Eilidh and I . . . you didn't know that?" Calum shook his head.

"Och, but he was the lad for a ploy. He joined the army the day the war started . . . aye, he lied about his age to get in." The old man drew on his pipe for a few minutes.

"Well," he resumed, "he was sent, like many another

fine lad, to fight the Japanese in the jungle. Rangi Singh here was a soldier too, at the time, and did they not find themselves marching shoulder to shoulder together. *A dhia*, but they were the hard times. Retreat, every day retreat, and themselves with the blood of warriors in their veins.

"They were in what you'd call the rearguard, covering the retreat of the main army. Rangi and my lad and a handful of others were ordered to hold a bridge for a few hours. They were told that reinforcements would be coming. Well, they held out for two days before they were over-run by the enemy. The lad and Rangi were the only survivors, and both of them wounded.

"Somehow the lad lasted a year in the prison camp, with Rangi tending him like a brother. In the end his wounds and the fever had the best of it and he died."

He paused. The fire crackled.

"When the war ended Rangi was released and, in time, he came to this country to make a living with the suitcase. Aye, Mr McKinnon, I owe a debt to Rangi that money can never repay."

The daylight had all but faded and the evening moths danced in the glow of the flickering fire.

"What happened to the reinforcements?" Calum asked. "Could they not get through?"

"Reinforcements, Mr McKinnon." The old man's words had the bite of the north wind. "There were never to be any reinforcements."

"But you said . . ." ventured Calum, puzzled.

"I said that they were ordered to hold the bridge and that reinforcements would come. To hold the brige was an order; the reinforcements . . . a promise. An order is to be obeyed, you'll understand. But a promise . . . Ah, Mr McKinnon, that's a matter of honour."

The old man thrust at the embers with a stick and his voice when he resumed, was heavy with contempt.

"The one who gave the order . . . and the promise, that gentleman didn't stop running till he was safe on board a ship heading for Australia, and Rangi and my lad and all the other lads were reported dead."

The old tinker sat staring into the embers, lost in his memories. Calum looked up to find that Rangi Singh's brown eyes were on him and his pearl white teeth showed in a slow widening smile. The puzzling events of the morning flooded back into Calum's mind.

"Rangi," Calum began, marshallng his thoughts. "This morning, at the Big House, when the Colonel looked you in the face . . ."

Two deep, dark pools, reflecting the fire's light, held Calum's gaze. Slowly the turbaned head nodded in assent.

Calum rose to his feet and staightened his tunic.

"Well, Eachunn, I'd better be on my way. I just looked in, in the passing, to say that there'll be no need for you to be shifting your camp. I believe the Colonel will not be bothering you . . . or anyone else on the island . . . very much from now on."

7

A Strange One

At least once every year Calum's wife Jean insisted on being taken to Glasgow to see the bright lights and the fine shops. He never failed to indulge her, just as long as she did not expect him to trail the streets too, and wise woman that she was she never did.

It was their custom, on such trips, to put up at the house of Jean's married cousin. When these two tireless bargain-hunters set course for the wonderland of the city centre, Calum would pass the time visiting a few old friends with a little something purchased at the licensed grocers in his pocket.

High on his list of calls was a small but decent tenement flat, situated in a not-too-select part of town where, in his 82nd year, resided Great Uncle Lachlan McKinnon. Among the first constables to have been stationed on Calum's island, Great Uncle Lachlan had been drawing his pension for well-nigh as long as Calum had seen service. Although restricted to the flat by advanced rhuematism and subjected to the benevolent tyranny of a widowed daughter, the old man's mind remained active and there was nothing he liked better than recalling things that were, in the days that are no more.

"Tell me, Calum," the old man queried, diluting a generous dram with a teaspoon measure of tap water, "are there Campbells still to be found at Ach a' Chaolais?"

"Aye," Calum confirmed, "there's a couple of young families, and an old man, but I've never clapped eyes on him."

"He wouldn't be called Andrew by any chance?" wondered the old man.

"I believe that's his name, right enough," replied Calum, glancing curiously across at his aged relative. "Did you know him in your time?"

"We met, on occasion," Great Uncle Lachlan answered evasively, "But as to knowing him, that would be a different matter." He was thoughtful for a spell before adding, "It's not from the islanders you'd be learning of him, you being an incomer, but as I was there the night it happened, and it requiring a police report, they had no option but to come to me. Now, how much of what they told me was fact and how much their own invention . . . och, *a dhia*, Calum, even to this day I can't rightly say. But as sure as this glass in my hand is empty," he looked pointedly at Calum's still healthy carry-out on the table before them, "this was the way of it".

Their glasses recharged and fresh coals on the fire, Great Uncle Lachlan related to Calum the history of the man known in the old tongue as *Aindrea Da-Shealladh* or, as they would have it in the English, Andrew of the Two Sights.

The summer and autumn of 1927 had been exceptionally kind to the islanders and the harvest was cut, gathered and safely stored before the fist chill caused peats to be kindled in the cotters' grates and the ocean-blue greyed beneath the darkening clouds of winter.

It was some moments before Lachlan was able to associate the hammering that had awakened him, with his own front door. Struggling from between the blankets, he threw on a greatcoat over his pyjamas and lit the paraffin lamp kept handy by the bed. By the light of the lamp held high, he discerned a woman on the doorsep, the tartan shawl which covered her head plucked and torn at by the gale which howled around the police station.

"All the other boats are back but my boys are still out there," the woman cried against the wind, turning her head to stare out into the darkness where the sea hurled itself on the rocks in one mounting, endless roar.

"Come you in out of the night," Lachlan invited, leading the way to his office. "Mrs Campbell, isn't it?" he said in recognition, as the woman uncovered her head.

"They were south of Sgeir Mhor when last seen, and the storm coming on them. There's no shelter there, Constable, and they should have been here long since."

Although the woman's voice was steady, Lachlan had seen the knuckles of her hands showing white where she clasped them before her. If new to the island itself, he was no stranger to the sea and its ways. A prolongued winding of the wall-telephone handle produced the drowsy voice of the night operator, then more speedily the ear of Seamus the lifeboat coxswain.

Lachlan was on the pier next morning when, the storm considerably abated, the lifeboat returned to harbour towing the Campbell's boat, or what remained of it.

Of the three Campbell brothers only two were brought ashore. The third, Andrew, had not been accounted for.

That evening the coxswain, accompanied by the two survivors, arrived at the police station to provide details of the disaster for Lachlan's official report. He opened the proceedings by expressing his sorrow to the Campbells for the tragic loss of their brother.

"Och, but it's kind of you to be saying that, Constable," Coll, the oldest brother acknowledged gravely. Then, somewhat less solemnly, he added, "It's maybe not lost that Andrew is, but just not here at the moment, as it were, if you're understanding me."

It was plain to the coxswain that the officer was far from understanding and, clearing his throat, he elected to intervene.

"To be knowing what the Campbell means, you would have to be of this island yourself, Constable, I'm thinking. For Andrew Campbell is not quite like the rest of us."

"Oh?" Lachlan puzzled, putting down his pen and giving the coxswain his full attention. "And in what way would that be now?"

"If you'll bear with me a little, Constable, I'll try to explain," the coxswain said, looking for and receiving the nodded permission of his two companions.

As the shadows lengthened in his tiny office, Lachlan learned from the coxswain the reason for the Campbells being in no hurry to begin grieving for their missing brother.

He was a small man, Andrew Campbell, slight of build and wan of complexion, whose childhood had been a succession of wearisome illnesses. His passage through school had been without note, with his views and opinions invariably ignored. Such indeed had been his apparent insignificance that he had soon come to accept his being present, but not quite, as normal.

He had two elder brothers, Coll and Alastair who, on leaving school, immediately secured berths on their father's fishing boat. Andrew had always assumed that he too, would follow in their steps and be a fisherman. And when his last term had finished he waited for his father to raise the subject of his joining the crew. He waited in vain. He would be on the pier when the boats came in and went out—a boat might be short of a man and he would be called. But he never was.

After a time Andrew stopped going to the harbour. At home his mother swept and dusted round him, cooked for the men coming home and washed their clothes, and his presence in the house seemed to cause her no inconvenience. To be fed, clothed and housed satisfied all his material needs and if life had more to offer he was not aware of it.

To fill his days Andrew took to walking the surrounding moors and hills, leaving behind him the strivings and ambitions which occupied the lives of those he knew. He would rise early and, with a piece of bread and cheese in his pocket, be well on his way before the sun's warmth had dried the dew on the heather. Following the sheep tracks on the lower slopes, he would make his way up the corries and round the crags, finding foot and hand holds in the lichen crevices, and when tired he would rest in the shelter of a rock and eat his meal.

At first he had felt alien in the silent world in which he moved, but increasingly he became aware of movement around him. If he sat quite still it would begin. He would be observed cautiously from a distance then, emboldened, stealthy rustlings would precede their appearance as they resumed their pursuits. Feather, fur and insect, all came to accept him as part of their day, sharing with him his bread and cheese, within hand's reach, without fear.

Excluded, as he had always been, from the society of his own kind, Andrew discovered amid the steeps and glens a new world in which all things, however insignificant, formed a related part in the oneness of creation. If this revelation did not immediately supply a purpose for his own existence, it did at least give some meaning to life itself.

One warm summer's day Andrew stretched his length in his favourite hollow, hands clasped behind his head, watching through half-closed eyes the tireless winging of the bees above the heather.

A sudden movement on the rim caught his attention. Beneath alert ears, two bright eyes like amber buttons held his gaze. Gone instantly was the lethargy which the steady droning of the bees had induced, replaced by a sensation of unease which was without reason for he had no sense of danger. Slowly, from the cover, a vixen rose and advanced to stand quivering before him, her eyes never for a moment straying from his. Little by little the disquiet within Andrew stilled, with the realisation that the anxiety he had felt had not been for himself, but for the vixen. Carefully he rose to his feet. The vixen turned from him and with one bound, she was up and away. Andrew followed the direction which she had taken, impelled by a feeling of urgency.

He was close to the summit of the hill when he came upon her again, where she sat panting, her tongue lolling. Wedged between two boulders, where a misjudged leap had landed him, was the vixen's mate, exhausted by his struggles to free himself.

The slightest parting of the rocks would have freed the animal, but the task, which would have been well within the capacity of his brothers, was, he feared, beyond his own powers. Nevertheless, taking hold of the lesser of the two boulders, he strained and hauled, but it moved not an inch.

As he braced his legs for one last, albeit hopeless attempt, the vixen sprang lightly on to the rock above him. Close to tears of frustration, Andrew looked up at the creature, imploring her forgiveness. The vixen's eyes, glowing like fanned embers in the darkness of the night, held him in her unswerving stare . . .

Unreal, as in a dream, yet ever nearer, Andrew heard the baying of the hounds and felt the trembling in his legs.

He was running, the pack at his heels. Through wood and brush he fled, twisting, turning, but the horror behind him was closing fast. They would be upon him soon, yelping, snarling, tearing at his flesh. Before him was a river, the rain-swollen flood racing towards a waterfall in a tumult of foam and spray, the safety of the opposite bank one impossible leap away. From deep within his being Andrew summoned that last reserve of strength that only terror can provide, and . . . gripping the boulder with both hands, Andrew heaved.

There was scarce a house in the village that did not have an empty place at the table when the call went out, "Your Country Needs You", and the Campbell home was no exception. Although the fishing was good, when the Kaiser's army marched to war, one of the first to volunteer was Andrew's brother Coll.

Short-handed by Coll's departure, Andrew was given a berth on his father's boat. He was quick to learn and to the surprise of all, he proved that, frail as he appeared, he was able to haul the nets in the cold of winter, stand his watch at the tiller and help discharge the night's catch of herring without showing those visible signs of fatigue which so clearly marked the faces of the other crewmen. Andrew, it was generally agreed, was certainly a strange one.

Little news of the events in France filtered back, and what there was was usually bad. It arrived, as often as not, in the form of a telegram or a letter, mud-soiled from Flanders, penned by the flickering light of a candle by an officer, old at twenty. There was no welcome for the postman in Andrew's village.

They were alone in the house, Andrew and his mother, the morning that the telegram arrived, buff coloured, impersonal. "It is with regret . . . missing, presumed dead." Stunned, his mother sank on to a chair at the kitchen table, staring vacantly into space, the telegram at her feet where it had fallen.

From his seat by the fire, Andrew had heard the knock at the door, had watched his mother open the envelope and seen the contents slip from her fingers. There was no need for him to read what had been written, her silence told the news. Slowly Andrew's eyelids closed . . .

. . . They played together on the shore, mother and child, built castles in the sand, and the sun shone for them. But the clouds gathered and in her ears was the rumble of thunder like the guns of war. And when the lightning forked, she saw that the sand was mud and the castles roofless churches, their flaming rafters pointing to the skies. It was by the redness of his hair that she recognised him, the child grown into man, among the litter of broken men, side by side, their faces gaunt beneath the bandages . . .

. . . Andrew's mother started in her chair, as though caught napping in the middle of the day and turning, found him smiling at her.

"He'd better be having my room when he comes home, mother," Andrew said, reaching for his jacket. "You can see the harbour from the window, and I'm thinking that the sight of the boats will be the mending of him."

Coll was ill, very ill, for a long time after he was shipped home and it was long after the victory bells had pealed and those men of the village who had survived had returned, that he was able to venture out and walk by the harbour that had been his life. He showed no inclination to talk of the war or of what he had seen or done, but would ask eagerly after this one or that one at the fishing and how the boats handled and were the herring still to be found where he'd known them to be.

Only once, when the others were at sea, as he sat staring into the glow of the fire and his mother baking at the kitchen table, did he speak of it. Not of the fighting or the killing but of the time he'd lain near to death in the field hospital. His mother rolled and kneaded the dough as he spoke and her heart beat the faster.

"I didn't know much about it when they brought me in," Coll said, stirring the coals with the poker. "There were people about me, but they were just white coats and voices far away. Then one morning the strangest thing happened, mother." He hesitated, glancing up at her as if undecided whether to continue. Her hands worked busily with the flour, her eyes cast down. Coll returned to prodding the fire. "If I told you who I thought I saw, just as clear as I see you now, standing there beside me and the face of him smiling down at me, you'd think me mad."

For some moments his mother worked the dough in silence, then without lifting her head she said quietly, "Might it have been Andrew, your brother?" The poker clattered against the grate as it fell from Coll's hand.

"Ah, they're back," she announced, as from the road came the voices of the others returning from the pier. "Put the kettle on the fire, Coll. They'll be needing a cup with the cold that's in it."

When Coll was well enough to return to the fishing, his

father made the decision to come ashore for good and gave the boat over to his sons. They fished well, the three brothers, and in time they married and had children of their own. That is Coll and Alastair did, for it seemed accepted that Andrew would remain single. Although their working lives were closely twined, Andrew remained, as he always had been, apart, somehow complete in himself.

The young ones, as they grew, were never out of his company and they would sit together on the shore or walk the hills, listening to the stories he would tell them.

"*A dhia*, Andrew and his fairy tales," their grandmother would scold when the house was filled with the clamour of their voices calling for him. "You shouldn't be believing all the daft things that Andrew tells you. It would fit you better to be at your school books and learning something useful."

It had been mild enough that evening when they set out from the harbour, and with sail and engine they had made fast progress to the fishing grounds. Although the herring were plentiful, it was still dark when Coll turned the bow towards home. For a time he had been aware of a freshening of the wind and had seen the white tips on the waves as the motion of the boat had increased. In the east, where the first tinge of morning should have shown, the sky was black with the weight of cloud over the sea.

It had been Coll's hope that, with the wind astern, they could make the shelter of the harbour on the run and, for a space, it seemed likely that they would succeed. But then the fury of the storm broke over them.

"Reef the sail." Coll's voice was barely heard above the risen gale as the first, towering wave crashed across their stern, almost wrenching the tiller from his grasp. Before the other two could reach the mast the sail was ripped asunder. Each surge hurled them forward and downwards into the trough, and each ascent became more laboured with the sea that filled the boat. The sail gone, the engine swamped, and the rudder useless against such a force, there was nothing they could do to save themselves.

In the forepart of the doomed vessel Andrew crouched by the splintered stump of the bowsprit, his eyes lightly closed, his face untroubled.

Consciousness came slowly to Coll, slumped across the tiller. He raised his head and looked around. A fading breeze blew lightly on his cheek, the sea scarcely giving motion to the planks beneath his feet. Above, the scudding clouds fled westwards before the dawning day, while the tattered sail flapped listlessly against the mast. At his feet his brother Alastair, dazed but unharmed, sought to free himself from the tangle of fallen rigging. Coll shivered, chilled by the touch of wet clothing against his skin.

"Andrew," Coll cried, struggling to his feet, his eyes searching the bow where, through the blinding spray, he had last glimpsed his youngest brother. There was no answer to his call.

"Well, Constable," the coxswain concluded, I'll have to be getting back to write my own report. Two saved and one . . . unaccounted for, is how I think I'll put it."

"But he can't stay unaccounted for ever, man," Lachlan protested, the blank report staring up at him from the desk.

"Och, dear me, no," the coxswain agreed. "It's the close family the Campbells are, so I'm not believing that Andrew would be causing his mother any undue worry. Anyway, we'll be knowing one way or the other soon, you can depend on it."

The coxswain rose to his feet along with the brothers

Campbell. "We'll be on our way now. The weather looks set for fair, so with luck, Constable, we'll both be getting our sleep tonight."

"How could he possibly have survived that night, alone in such a sea?" Calum asked, when the old man had finished speaking. But the question remained unanswered, for Great Uncle Lachlan was fast asleep in his chair.

8

Calum's Honoured Guest

Chief Inspector Twatt drummed his fingers on the desk in his Sub Divisional office at Oban as he awaited a telephone connection with Constable Calum McKinnon's island station. Contact, in any form, with his far-flung subordinate, invariably had an adverse effect on the Chief Inspector, and his day had barely begun. The telephone bell trilled.

"Constable McKinnon here, sir," the well known voice reported.

"Ah, McKinnon, I wanted a word with you about the elections," the Chief Inspector began, his free hand groping in the top drawer of the desk for a packet of stomach settlers.

"Och aye, Inspector," Calum acknowledged, "myself was thinking that I'd just be voting again for that young fellow over yonder in Dumbarton—dashed if I can mind his name, but I'm sure he's doing a grand job."

"Dumbarton?" the Chief Inspector echoed. "What are you talking about, man?"

"The police federation elections next week, sir," informed Calum.

"The federation . . ." the Chief Inspector faltered, then gathering himself, "dammit, McKinnon, I'm talking about the General Election this week."

"Oh, that election," Calum's tone lost much of its enthusiasm. "Aye, sir, you were saying?"

Deep lines of anguish creased the Chief Inspector's face, as a sharp twinge in the pit of his stomach heralded the reactivation of a, for some time past, dormant ulcer. "As you may, or may not know, McKinnon, the sitting member, the Hon Cuthbert Wellindowed, a gentleman of excellent qualities, is being challenged this time by a Miss McLean of the Progressive Crofter's Party, whatever that is."

"That will be Sheena McLean," interrupted Calum, knowledgeably. "Her cousin Archie's the postman here."

"You know this woman?" asked the Chief Inspector.

"Yes indeed, to be sure, sir, replied Calum. "Her people have a rented croft here, or rather, they had, until the land was bought up by one of those finance companies down in London and given over to pheasant shooting. She appealed to Mr Wellindowed at the time, but he told her that the sport would be good for the tourist trade."

"You can depend on it, McKinnon, our MP knows what he's talking about," crooned the Chief Inspector.

"Och, I don't doubt that, sir," agreed Calum. "Is it not he himself that's coming here every year for the shooting . . . as a sort of "guest" of the new owners, you might say. And where else would he be staying but in the cottage that the McLeans were put out of?"

"You're remarkable well informed, McKinnon," the Chief Inspector said icily.

"It's good of you to say so, sir," thanked Calum. "I feel that it's my simple duty to keep abreast of things, as it were."

"Yes, quite," the Chief Inspector quickly returned to the subject in hand. "Mr Wellindowed will be crossing over today for a "meet the people" tour of your island, and he will be addressing a public meeting in the village hall in the evening. I believe your other candidate will share the platform with him." For the umteenth time he scanned the shift-sheet before him, with the same negative result. "Unfortunately, I've no one available to send over. So, McKinnon, it's all up to you. I don't want any "incidents", if you understand me."

"Certainly not, Inspector," Calum assured. "You can rely on me."

From bitter experience, Calum's ready acceptance of the responsibility did little to comfort the Chief Inspector. But as he had always led a blameless life, he felt justified in hoping for divine intervention.

"And, McKinnon," he recalled with distaste his last visit to the island, "see that your uniform is pressed."

Later that morning, Constable McKinnon stationed himself on the fringe of the party faithful who were on the pier awaiting the docking of the mainland ferry. From the head of the gangway, the Hon Cuthbert Wellindowed MP gallantly raised his hat in acknowledgement of the Hip-Hip-Hurrahs that greeted his appearance. As he stepped ashore, he was instantly surrounded by his hand-shaking supporters.

That the pier workers showed little interest in the proceedings caused Calum no great surprise—for by long established custom, matters politic fell within the province of the island's gentlefolk. From the days of his childhood, Calum recalled sitting by his father on the hard wooden benches in his village hall listening, with little comprehension, to the lofty outpourings of visiting gentlemen who, in appearance, differed little from the morning's arrival.

The bright rosettes, pinned to the tweed jackets and velvet dresses of the lairds and their ladies on the platform, had made them seem to him like guests at a wedding to which neither he nor his father had been invited. He had come, with the passage of years, to better understand why his father and a number of other crofters around him, had sat immobile during such events, their calloused hands clasped before them, their gaze fixed stoically on their boots.

Calum awoke from his reverie, when the babble of politely excited voices gave way to the revving of motor car engines, as the MP and his cortege drove off in the direction of his campaign headquarters, the laird's house at Kildallick.

As the distinguished visitor had appeared not ungratified by the enthusiasm of his reception, Calum concluded that the Chief Inspector could not in any way classify the demonstration as an "incident". So his duty faithfully performed, he departed the pier for the police station, the pleasing thought of lunch gaining prominence in his mind.

In the kitchen of the police house his wife Jean was busy at the cooker.

"You've just missed Sheena McLean," she said. "She dropped in with her election pamphlet. *A dhia*, Calum, but she was looking that weary, and her knocking doors from one end of the island to the other. Her cousin, Archie's been giving her a hand, but with that old car of his for ever breaking down, she's been on her feet most of the time."

Calum picked up the pamphlet and as he read through, it was as though he was again listening to the very words of his own father those many years ago in the peat glow of their croft. Ailing and prematurely old, his eyes had kindled bright, not just with the fever, but with the smouldering anger, his spirit frustrated from birth by an ancient system of land tenure.

"Oh, and Calum," Jean added, "the Chief Inspector phoned to say that Mr Wellindowed would be needing to use the police station this evening."

"Did he now?" said Calum, looking up with interest.

"Aye, it seems that his tour of the island will take him up to nearly the start of the public meeting. So, as he won't have time to go back to Kildallick House to change his clothes, he's going to do it here, with us being handy to the hall. His things will be brought over later and you've to see them hung up properly so they won't be crushed."

Calum digested this piece of news, along with a generous portion of fresh run salmon which had found its way from the river to his back doorstep in the early hours of the morning—a not unusual occurrence when the word was out that the estate gamekeeper was at the bottle.

As Calum had calls to make at various parts of the island that day, he had several sightings of the Hon Cuthbert's cavalcade as it progressed regally from hamlet to hamlet. The sole glimpse he had of the Progressive Crofter's candidate, was a rear view of her as she trudged up a steep farm track, while by the roadside, her cousin's car sat immobile, the bonnet up and steam erupting from the radiator, like a volcano at full blast.

On his return to the station, Calum's wife informed him that the gentleman's clothes had been delivered and that she had hung them up in the cell. With the heater switched on she had considered it an ideal changing-room, the possibility of it being required for its intended purpose being judged non-existent.

Curiosity guided Calum's steps down the cell passage. "Well now, is that not the splendid sight," he admired aloud as, cap pushed back and hands on hips, he gazed at the apparelled coat-hanger suspended from a hook in the cell. No Highland chief, at the summit of his glory, could have aspired to the quality of the kilt, hose, sporran and velvet jacket which had been prepared for the adornment of the Hon Cuthbert Wellindowed.

The polished Daimler that glided to a halt before the police station a bare 15 minutes before the public meeting in the village hall was due to start, disembarked the laird and the sitting member.

"On the toes, McKinnon," the laird boomed at the seated Constable McKinnon, as his ample form steam-rollered the office, his forefinger pounding the face of a gold-chained pocket-watch. "Cutting it damned fine, can't you see."

"Everything's ready for you, sir," Calum addressed the honourable member, as he emerged from behind the laird.

"Splendid, splendid," thundered the laird, heading back towards the door. "Can't wait, old man. Still things to see to," he fired off in the direction of the Hon Cuthbert. "See to things, McKinnon, see to things." And he was gone.

"It's been a pleasant enough day," remarked Calum, genially, rising laboriously to his feet, "though I'm thinking there'll be frost before morning."

"Where are my clothes, man?" was the Hon Cuthbert's response, weather forecasts seemingly coming low on his list of priorities.

"Och, they're safe as can be," assured Calum. "If you'll just follow me, sir." He led the way down the passage and into the cell.

The Hon Cuthbert eyed his surroundings with obvious distaste. "If this is your idea of humour, Constable. I assure you, it's not mine. nor, would I suggest, that of the Chief Inspector."

"Well, sir, it's more private than the front office. You never know who might walk in there," Calum pointed out.

"Don't you think your own house might be an improvement?" came the suggestion.

"Not really, sir," Calum denied. "I'm decorating and there's wet paint everywhere."

"Oh, very well," snapped the Hon Cuthbert testily, throwing off his jacket and slackening his tie. Calum's not inconsiderable frame filled the doorway, an amiable smile on his face.

"What are you ogling at?" demamded the honourable member, about to down his trousers. "Remove yourself. And close the door behind you."

Calum hesitated for a moment and seemed inclined to raise a point of order.

"Are you deaf," the Hon Cuthbert glared at his unwanted observer. "Get out, and close that confounded door."

Obediently, Calum stepped backwards and swinging the heavy metal-faced door, he retired to the front office, determined finally to attend to a dusty pile of Force Standing Orders. With commendable dedication, he applied himself to following the departmental meanderings of pink, white and green forms.

So absorbed did he become in the ways of these colourful documents that it was some time before he was distracted by the muffled sounds which filtered up from the cell passage. Pausing only to withdraw and replace the superceded order, he made his way to the souce of the disturbance.

Dropping the small, hinged trap in the centre of the cell door, Calum bent down and found himself eye-ball to eye-ball with the Hon Cuthbert Wellindowed, resplendent in full Highland dress.

"Did you want something, sir?" Calum enquired solicitously.

"There's no blasted handle on this door," the occupant of the cell declared.

Calum pondered on this novel piece of information. "No, sir. There wouldn't be, otherwise the prisoners would just be walking out whenever they had a mind for it."

"Then turn the handle on your side and let me out of here," the honourable member hissed through clenched teeth.

Without even having to examine the stout metal structure, Calum was able to state, with complete certainty, "There isn't one on this side either. It's a key we'd have to be using."

"Use it," the captive's voice was low and full of menace.

"Ah, now sir, there's a wee difficulty there," informed Calum, stroking his chin. "The thing is, sir, the Chief Inspector's had this fine new lock fitted, which operates as soon as the door is shut, you'll understand, but he hasn't got round to sending me the key as yet. I'm expecting it in the post any day now."

Although not prudish by any means, Calum's sensitivities were shocked by the flood of invective which assailed his ears from the interior of the cell. Manfully, he bore the verbal assault until, over-stepping the accepted bounds of propriety, the Hon Cuthbert hinted darkly of irregularities in the wedded state of his custodian's long deceased parents.

Showing exemplary self control Calum excused himself, pleading more pressing duties, and closing the hatch on the apoplectic honourable member, he retired with dignity to the office. Donning his cap and restoring the polish on the toe caps of his boots by rubbing them vigorously on the backs of his trousered legs, Calum headed for the village hall.

When he arrived the public meeting had been under way

for some time. On the platform, the Progressive Crofter's candidate was on her feet, driving home her policy, point after point, to a receptive packed house. Beside her at the table, the laird of Kildallick sat slumped, the all too empty chair of the Hon Cuthbert next to him.

Calum made his unobtrusive way round to the back of the stage and taking advantage of a prolonged burst of applause, he moved in behind the chairman, whispered in his ear, then withdrew again to the body of the hall. The grey-haired schoolmaster, whose undenied contempt for all forms of government, religions, and like human pretensions, made him the ideal neutral chairman, rose to his feet.

"Ladies and gentlemen, if I could have your attention," he intoned. Their attention he instantly had, for few present had not, at one time, been his pupil and classroom habits die hard. "I have to announce that Mr Wellindowed has been . . . unavoidably detained, and will not be able to join us tonight." In general, the meeting displayed little disappointment at this news, and Sheena McLean launched again into her speech.

The following morning, in the Oban Sub Division's 'holy of holies'—Chief Inspector Pratt's carpeted office—Ian Anderson, accelerated promotion success and man-with-a-future settled just a trifle self-consciously behind the boss's desk and marvelled at his good fortune. Bright-eyed, his fresh young face as yet unlined by the burdens of responsibility, inspector's pips still shiny new on his unbowed shoulders, there he was—master of all he surveyed, and that seemingly for an indefinite period.

Although a comparative newcomer to the division, he knew of course of the Chief Inspector's recurring stomach trouble. But the sudden collapse and removal to hospital of his unfortunate superior the previous evening, following a telephone call from the principal laird of one of the islands, had been an event quite unforseen. What, he wondered, could have been the import of the call, which had so dramatically advanced his career. He reached for the phone.

"Yes, sir," the bar officer answered him.

"Put me through to the police station on Innis Rosaich," the inspector instructed. "It's a Constable McKinnon that's there, isn't it?"

"Aye, sir . . . er, Calum McKinnon," the bar officer admitted, the paternal instinct to protect his fledgling boss from so early a perilous encounter behind his hesitation. "I'm putting you through now, sir."

As the young inspector sat awaiting his connection, a heavy cloud enveloped the face of the sun, dulling the bright rays of morning light streaming through the tastefully curtained window of his office. But the portent failed to register with him.

9
Och-nan-Och, Calum

Jean's gold-rimmed spectacles appeared above the newspaper that she was holding at full-stretch before her.

"Who's going to win this time, Calum?" she asked anxiously.

"Well," opined her husband seated opposite her at their kitchen table, spooning down a soft-boiled egg while trying to follow the football results on the back page, "on their present form I'd say Aberdeen . . . but then again, Rangers still have a game in hand, so . . ."

"Och, don't be daft," Jean snapped. "I'm talking about this strike that's going on, over there on the mainland."

"Oh that," Calum replied with an indifferent shrug of the shoulders. "I've no idea. They'll just have to find some kind of compromise, I expect." Calum was a great believer in compromise, for it had served him well during his long years as a policeman and never more so perhaps, than on his present one-man island station.

"Don't you be troubling yourself about it, Jean," he advised, rising up and buttoning his tunic. "Apart from the schoolmaster, the minister and himself up at the Big House, it's peat we use here and there's no shortage of that on this island, thank God. Anyway, I'm not thinking that they even know that we exist, over there in England, nor in Glasgow for that matter."

Somewhat reassured, Jean lowered her paper to observe the daily ritual of her husband searching for the keys of his panda car. "Try the sideboard, Calum," she hinted with infinite patience.

In his tiny office, Constable McKinnon balefully contemplated a plump pack of Road Traffic Amendments gathering dust on his desk. What, he speculated, would have happened to Moses if he hadn't had the foresight to drop and break those tablets, etched with the principal Act, while on his way down from yon mountain? Would the poor sod have spent the rest of his days trailing up to the summit to fetch endless revised editions? The assumption, Calum pessimistically considered, that God would have got it right the first time just didn't hold water, for after all, hadn't he made man in his own image?

Calum made the not too difficult decision to leave the ammendments for a rainy day and quitting the office, he set course for the pier. On his arrival at the harbour he was to make the discovery that the anonymity of his island was not as absolute as he had previously suggested.

The visit of the twice weekly ferry from the mainland, even in the grey days of winter, was an important event. If few tourists braved the crossing, the ferry remained a lifeline for the necessities and little luxuries which made their lives tolerable. As he arrived Calum observed a stranger descending the gangway. The man was dressed in a heavy overcoat and wore dark-tinted spectacles beneath the snap brim of a felt hat, his only luggage a bulging briefcase. The visitor was welcomed by Big Angus, the democratically elected spokesman for the island's three-man-strong Amalgamated Union of Rope Catchers and Bollard Minders.

In spite of a cutting wind from the North, a full turnout of the membership had assembled to confer earnestly with the stranger. Calum eased off the car's handbrake, allowing it to roll forward a few feet to obtain a better view of the proceedings. A proposal appeared to have been made, which was seconded by a solemn nod from Big Angus and passed unanimously by hands being removed from pockets and raised briefly in the air.

The discussion having ended, seemingly to the satisfaction of all interested parties, a course of direct action immediately followed. Purposefully, the meeting transferred itself to an ancient, steam-operated crane, situated at the far end of the pier. With interest, Calum watched the stranger extract from his briefcase a length of chain and an imposing padlock, which he then employed to secure the crane's gear-lever to a convenient strut.

His mission fulfilled, he vigorously pumped Big Angus' hand, bestowed a well-done-lad slap on the backs of the others and hurried back up the gangway of the about to depart ferry, his immediate goal, without a doubt, the saloon bar and a double of anything to restore the circulation.

Shielded by a permanent stow of irreparably damaged fish boxes from the vulgar gaze of the commonality and in like manner from burdened travellers in search of assistance with their luggage, stood a wooden shack, the door of which bore the legend, Union Branch Headquarters. Calum coughed discreetly before opening the door and effecting a casual entry.

All credit to the swiftness of the men's reflexes, there was not a penny piece to be seen on the upturned orange box they were sitting at. However the exciting game of Snap which was being played did not and was not really meant to deceive him. With an innocent show of interest, Calum stood over them, a bulky figure in official garb.

It was Big Angus who cracked first.

"The pier's been blacked, Constable McKinnon," he blurted out. "Yon was the Union's secretary from Glasgow and we've agreed that no coal's to be landed on this pier till the dispute's been settled."

"Aye, I was thinking that it might be something of the likes," acknowledged Calum, " and the puffer due in tomorrow, is she not, Angus?" he added by way of conversation, imparting a light but significant squeeze to the shoulder of the player on his left who he had spotted slipping a card from the bottom of the pack.

"She is that," confirmed Big Angus. "And she'll be wasting her time too, for without us she can't tie up or discharge, and we will be witholding our labour. An official strike, mind you, Constable," he hastened to add, "with the Union's blessing."

Mid-morning the following day, Calum was present to witness the arrival of the coal puffer from the mainland. Ranged along the edge of the pier was Big Angus and his two stalwarts, holding aloft plackards intimating the closure of the port.

The puffer with its cargo of high grade anthracite stood off a little from the pier wallowing in the swell like a gorged seagull while Big Angus and the skipper exchanged insults. It is a well-known fact that the language of the Gael, since its inception in the Garden of Eden, has developed through the ages a subtleness in implying another's worthlessness infinitely more devastating than the crude, four-lettered expletives of its less mature Anglo-Saxon cousin.

Calum set a match to his pipe and prepared to enjoy

what promised to be a truly memorable performance. Sadly his enjoyment was short lived. With the principals barely warming to their parts, a shooting-brake drew up beside him.

"What's the hold up?" Hamish the barman from the hotel asked, winding down the car window. Trying not to miss a syllable of what was being said on stage, Calum explained the situation.

"Not going to land at all?" the barman exclaimed. "*A dhia*, but yourself will have to do something about that, Constable."

"Och dear me, no," Calum declined with an air of righteousness. "Who am I to be interfering with the rights and privileges of the working man?"

"You'll be knowing about the rights of the working man soon enough, Constable, when he discovers that there's no a dram to be had on the whole island." There was terror in Hamish's voice as he spoke and the colour quite drained from his cheeks. "Our six month supply of whisky's on board that damned puffer and not so much as a drop left up at the hotel.

Calum had weathered many a crisis in the service, but the prospect of a totally dry island momentarily unnerved him. Civil riot could well be the least of it, and unilateral cessation from the crown not out of question. Furiously Calum puffed at his pipe.

"Come on Hamish," he said at length. "You can row me out to the puffer. I'll need to have a word with the skipper."

On his return ashore, Calum beckoned to the strikers to join him in their hut. When all were assembled, he carefully locked the door and snibbed the window. Then, without preamble, he gave them the facts of the situation straight from the shoulder, man to man.

"*Mo creach*, Constable McKinnon, what's to be done,"

Big Angus wailed. "If we let the puffer dock yon man will be back with a dozen others and they'll lynch us for sure."

"Aye, that they would," Calum agreed, already imagining with loathing, the mountain of paperwork that would arise from a triple lynching. Clearly the choice facing Big Angus and his men was between suffering grevious bodily harm at the hands of their brother unionists from across the sea, or from the native born when it was discovered that it was they who were the cause of the drought on the island. Neither option had much to recommend it.

"When I was out at the puffer," Calum remarked casually, "I was saying to the skipper that it's the fair old age that she must be now and what with her having the riveted plates, she'd be taking water in the hold, as like as not."

"Och aye, it's more than likely," concurred Big Angus, the relevence of the aging problems of an antique puffer to his own decidedly uncertain future, beyond him.

"And if she's to stand off here till the strike's over, and her filled to the gunwales with coal," Calum carried his theory to its logical conclusion, "they'll not be able to pump her out, will they?"

The soundness of Calum's reasoning could not be faulted and there descended on the company a depressing silence, disturbed only by the steady tick of the wall-clock and an occasional, *Och-nan-Och* of despair from the condemned trio.

The certainty of being held responsible for the puffer foundering with all hands gained prominence in Big Angus' mind over what was, after all, only the likelihood that he would be strung from a tree.

"We could always beach her," he suddenly exclaimed. Glancing up at Constable McKinnon, he received by the merest hint of a wink, confirmation of his inspired proposal.

"*A dhia*, but it's the sharp mind that's at you, Angus," Calum said. "I wonder why myself didn't think of that?"

The tide was at its peak when, with the wholehearted assistance of Big Angus and his men, the puffer was grounded on a sandy beach a half mile south of the harbour. As the vessel was round bottomed with little in the way of a keel, there was only a slight tilt to starboard when the tide receded to leave her high and dry.

"Well Skipper, she'll be safe as houses now," Big Angus assured, breathing heavily from the unaccustomed labour. As if in afterthought, he added. "As we're here anyway, we might as well unload the order for the hotel and drop it off on our way home. Man, but is it not lucky we have the van with us, and it fine and handy up there on the road."

"It's mighty thoughtful that you are to be offering," the skipper gratefully acknowledged, "but I'm afraid that won't be possible."

"Why ever not?" Big Angus demanded to know, just a shade threatening.

"Och, myself would be glad to see the back of them," the skipper was quick to affirm, "but you see, the boxes for the hotel are stowed in the starboard locker down there in the hold. To be getting at them, and her with the wee list and all, you would have to be taking the coal out first . . . and that would be breaking your strike, would it not?"

The two non-office bearers turned to give their leader their undivided attention. Although Big Angus was an imposing figure of a man, his followers could by no yardstick be described as lightweights. The expressions on their faces conveyed none of those admirable qualities of tolerance and fair play for which their island race is justifiably renowned.

"Correct me if I'm wrong," Calum attempted to forestall

the impending unpleasantness, "but is it not the pier that your man put out of bounds?"

"*Mo chreach*, but you have the right of it there, Constable," Big Angus gladly grasped the lifebelt which Calum had tossed him. "Not a word he said about not unloading on the beach. And another thing," he persisted, the still not quite convinced looks he was receiving from his men sharpening his wits wonderfully, "the tide will be going back from now on and we'll never float her off with the weight that's in her."

The sense of what he had said and the pressing need to see the hotel restocked was winning the day for the big man. "Come on lads, lets get to it." He was over the rail in a trice and scrambling up the deck towards the hatch, the membership following close in his wake.

It was near to closing time that evening when Calum, his uniform tunic replaced by an old sports jacket, strolled down to the hotel and stepped through the swing doors of the public bar. Installed at a corner table, he was pleased to see, was the full complement of the local branch of the Amalgamated Rope Catchers and Bollard Minders. In appearance they were not unlike the Black and White Minstrels of a bygone age, for it was many a long day since they had had to shovel a puffer empty by hand.

At the counter, Hamish the barman noticed Calum eyeing his freshly stocked gantry.

"Thanks to Big Angus and the boys," Hamish chuckled, vigorously polishing a tumbler. "Arrived half and hour ago they did, with the whole order and it's myself that was glad to see them." Hamish's face took on a haunted look. "If the lads had come in here tomorrow night, with nothing here but empty bottles, and it Saturday . . . *Ochon a righ,* it just doesn't bear thinking about."

Calum crossed to the corner table. The threesome, their teeth pearly white in the blackness of their faces, grinned him to a seat. "I was just thinking," he remarked, guaging the glasses on the table to be trebles at the very least; an impressive token of the barman's appreciation, "about all the valuable coal lying out there on the beach . . . from the point of view of security, you'll understand. I'd willingly keep an eye on it myself, but with the inspector, over there in Oban, thinking overtime a sinful word, it's yourselves will have to sit by it, day and night, till the strike's over."

As this wholly unforeseen complication appeared to have deprived his listeners of speech, Calum elected to continue. "Unless, that is, you could think of some suitable place to store it, under lock and key, of course."

"Aye, that would be a way out, right enough," agreed Big Angus, rubbing the bristles on his chin, the prospect of spending so much as one night shivering on the beach little to his liking.

"As there's only the schoolmaster, the minister and himself up at the big house who need the stuff for their boilers, it's themselves who'll be having proper cellars, with locks and all, for keeping it. If you were to see them first thing in the morning, I'm not thinking that you would have much trouble persuading them to take it off your hands," Calum confidently prophesised, rising to his feet.

As was his custom, Calum had a last prowl round the pier to satisfy himself that all was in order before heading home for the night. Included on his check list was the chain and padlock that secured the crane and proclaimed Big Angus' solidarity with the cause. Calum gave the padlock a firm pull. It did not give an inch.

10

A Wee Misunderstanding

In his mainland office the Chief Inspector reached for the ringing telephone.

"Yes, indeed, sir," he answered the enquiry from the Superintendent at the other end of the line. "They left on the early boat and I can assure you, sir, Constable McKinnon has *not* been notified."

A further query from his superior required a moment's thought. "I'd say," he replied guardedly, "with an allegation of incompetence we'd be on fairly safe ground." Sensing that his recommendation had fallen short of his listener's expectations, he quickly increased the stakes. "Or perhaps, neglect of duty might be more appropriate, wouldn't you say, sir?" This improved bid appeared to satisfy the Superintendent and, as the Chief Inspector replaced the receiver, the prospect of being finally and for ever quit of Constable Calum McKinnon he found much to his liking.

Across the sheltered waters of the Firth of Lorn and beyond the high misty mountains of the Isle of Mull, Constable Calum McKinnon guarded, watched and patrolled his island domain blissfully unaware that plans were afoot in high places, to compass his downfall. At the very hour when the details of the plot were being finalised, the subject of the conspiracy was closeted in his police office, with an incensed Major Cruncher, the sporting tenant of Drambigun Estate.

"Dash it all, McKinnon," the major fumed, "the March Pool held at least a dozen prime salmon yesterday evening and today, not a one. Got some chaps from the regiment over, and not a blasted fish to be had. A poor show McKinnon, loss of face, don't you see?"

Calum opened his mouth to speak, but the Major had not finished.

"And don't dare to suggest that they've just moved on upstream. You know as well as I do, there isn't enough water in the runs."

"I wasn't thinking that at all, sir," Calum hastened to reassure his visitor. "Myself and the gillie had a look early this morning and there's not a doubt that it's poached the pool was. From the footprints in the mud, I would be judging there were three of them at it."

"Good work, McKinnon," the major brightened visibly. "All we have to do now is catch the blighters on the job." The major squared his shoulders and, for a gentleman raised from birth to command, he made an offer praiseworthy in its humility. "I and my fellow officers are at your disposal in this matter, Constable. Use us as you will."

Although not insensible of the honour done him, Calum

was aware of the pitfalls inherent in the major's proposition. "It's grateful I am to you sir. But as it's a police matter, it would be best left to myself and the gillie, who knows every inch of the river."

The major took Calum's diplomatic rebuff in good part and soon took his leave, wishing the officer good fortune and conveying the impression that he was resigned to allowing the legally constituted authority to do its duty without the support of Her Majesty's armed forces.

That afternoon, when the tide was on the flow, Calum and the gillie, whose proportions quite dwarfed the not insignificant dimensions of the officer, inspected the lower beats of the river.

"*Chan'eil e cho dona, a Chaluim,*" relief showed on the gillie's face as he pronounced the situation not as serious as might have been expected.

"*Seadh, tha iad a'tighinn fhathast,*" Calum was happy to agree with the gillie, for it was plain to see that fresh-run fish were still entering the pools to rest and adjust to the change from salt to river water, before continuing on to the upper reaches.

"I would not be surprised but you'll be having visitors on the river this night," he opined, glancing up at the big man by his side. The ominous silence that followed he took for assent. In affairs affecting the gillie's river, Calum knew that he had to tred warily.

"With the closeness that's in it, and not a stir of wind, it might be that I'll have the fancy for a bit of a stroll this evening to get a breath of fresh air, as it were."

For a space the gillie weighed Calum's overt proposal, then advised that it was not unusual for a breeze to pick up from the sea, around midnight as a rule, and that a patch of raised shrubland, situated between the March and the Minister's Pool, was as good a spot to benefit from it as any.

Major Cruncher kept a tight reign on his men, surprise being the first principle of attack.

"They know the drill, Charles?" he whispered to the young lieutenant, all aquiver at his elbow.

"Absolutely,sir," came the dry-mouthed confirmation. "Clandestine approach . . . on the given signal, chge, and immobilise the enemy before he can retaliate."

"Splendid," acknowledged the major. "And Charles, gag the blighters, don't want them concocting an alibi before debriefing . . . what?"

By moonlight, the crouched figures crept stealthily through the bracken towards the unsuspecting foe.

"Now," the major's bellow shattered the silence. Like tigers, they launched themselves at their designated targets; two to each of three humped sleeping bags. In seconds it was over; the sleeping bags coil-roped and knotted, their occupants wild-eyed, gagged and *hors de combat*.

"Mission accomplished, sir," the young lieutenant reported, snapping to attention, right hand smartly up to the brim of his deerstalker hat, one, two, three— down—one, two, three—thumbs in line with the seems of his plus-fours. "No casualties, three prisoners taken, sir."

"First class, chaps," the major congratulated, smiling his pleasure to all concerned. "A credit to the regiment." Confirmation that life was not extinct in the sleeping bags, he achieved by prodding each in turn with his walking-stick, receiving in return an indignant, albeit, muted response.

"Fetch the transport, Charles, and get loaded up," instructed the major. "And the booty, Charles," he added, indicating a well-filled plastic bag and a sodden net on the ground by the prisoners. "Don't forget the booty."

In the wee small hours of the morning the light still burned in the office of Constable Calum McKinnon. His uniform jacket draped over the back of a chair, he was laboriously two-fingering a report on the typewriter, when he heard a vehicle draw up outside. The engine stopped and a murmur of voices preceeded a summoning knock on the office door. Wearily Calum rose to investigate but before he had covered half the distance to the door, it was thrown open and Major Cruncher strode in.

"Good morning, sir," Calum greeted his visitor with an enthusiasm which he certainly did not feel.

"It most certainly is," concurred the major. "Got something here that should put stripes on your arm, McKinnon. Don't look for thanks, of course. Compliments of the regiment." Then, turning back to the door. "Bring them in, chaps," he invited.

Calum was forced to retreat behind his counter as, into the office, trooped a column of men. What was then propped against his wall he identified as three nylon sleeping bags, tightly bound with ropes. Singular as this was in itself, what unnerved Calum was the human head which protruded from the neck of each bag.

"The poachers," the major announced with a casual sweep of the hand in the direction of his muffled productions, from which three pairs of eyes, awesome in the intensity of their malevolence, stared back at him. Then, tapping with his walking stick, a large plastic bag which had been dumped on the floor, he continued. "The evidence . . . four decent salmon, one sea-trout and of course the net.

From the look of anticipation on the major's face, Calum

knew that a response was expected from him, and that immediately.

"Ahaa . . ." he forced, and considering the turmoil in his mind and the sinking feeling which he was experiencing in the pit of his stomach, it was a worthy effort.

Assuming that emotions generated by gratitude had robbed the poor fellow of speech, the major pressed on. In a preamble to his account of the circumstances leading to the apprehension of the felons, he made it clear that to have meekly stood by while others did their bit would not have been in the tradition of the regiment.

"An ambush by night, Constable, just our cup of tea," the major warmed to his subject as Calum sank limply into a chair. "Zero one one five, reconnoitered river from mouth to March Pool. Enemy patrol, three in number, spotted on far bank stowing booty into black plastic bag. Zero one three zero, enemy patrol withdrew in close order, travelling east. Crossed river and pursued at discreet distance. Zero one four six, enemy seen to bed down, no guard posted."

The Major paused, face flushed, breathing heavily. "By thunder, I'd have them on the carpet for that."

Composure re-established, he concluded. "Zero two zero zero, successful assault on enemy position, three prisoners and a quantity of booty taken."

But for a spasm of strangulated wheezing coming from one of the upstanding sleeping bags, following the gallant Major's report, it would remain a matter of mere conjecture how long Calum's state of mental paralysis could have lasted. Activated by the appalling prospect of a sudden death inquiry, originating in his own office, he hurriedly removed the gags.

It was not until the de-gagged sleeping-bags had exhausted their store of pent-up obsenities on the company in general and basely vilified the military personnel in particular, that they volunteered the information that they themselves were police officers; a sergeant and two constables by rank. A search of a rucksack, which they had with them, produced warrant cards which confirmed their identity beyond all reasonable doubt. The ropes untied, the three emerged from confinement, maintaining what dignity was possible in string vests and underpants.

The first pale light of dawn had filtered through Calum's office window, before he was in possession of all the relevant facts. His Superintendent on the mainland, a man whose complete confidence, Calum sensed, he had never quite won, had apparently received information that three previously convicted poachers had crossed on the island ferry. Deviously, the Superintendent had imported the officers from an outside police division and had despatched them, in plain clothes, to the island with orders to apprehend the criminals in the act.

Prior to their departure, they had been counselled that under no circumstances were they to make contact with the resident constable, Calum McKinnon. In order not to draw attention to themselves in the village, the undercover officers had taken sleeping-bags with them and established a camp in the vicinity of the river.

In the small hours they had come upon the poachers, who were about to depart with a number of salmon that they had just netted. As luck would have it, the miscreants got clean away in the darkness. However the fish they had abandoned in their haste were taken possession of by the officers and removed to their camp site, to be handed over to the landowner in the morning.

The successful outcome of this assignment, Calum was not slow to appreciate, would have so undermined the islanders' confidence in him, that his transfer to a less responsible post on the mainland would have been inevitable.

"Dashed poor performance," the major addressed the underclothed officers critically. "You let the blighters escape, then skulk about like confounded bandits yourselves."

The absence of any apology form the major, compounded by his unjust censure, caused the vested sergeant to see red. "You sir—all of you," he glared venomously at the military detachment, "are guilty of assaulting police officers while in the execution of their duty."

"I say, steady on, old chap," the major remonstrated.

"I must warn you that I'm about to make a charge against you." Word perfect, the sergeant intoned the obligatory caution, "You needn't say anything in reply, but anything you do say . . ."

Realising that the man was in deadly earnest, Calum saw fit to intervene. "There is of course sergeant, the wee matter of the salmon and the net to be considered."

"The what?" snapped the sergeant, baffled by the relevance of Calum's interruption to the serious charge he was then laying.

"The bag of salmon you had with you when the major made his . . . och now, what did they call it at the police college? . . . aye, I remember, his citizen's arrest."

"His citizen's what?" the sergeant hissed.

"Arrest, sergeant," Calum repeated. "You see, the major is the tenant of the river and therefore the legal owner of those salmon. As he plainly doesn't know you from Adam, I'm not thinking that he will have been giving you permission to be in possession of them."

"Not blasted likely," came the major's emphatic confirmation.

"You'll be understanding my problem, sergeant," Calum persisted, his honest features showing genuine concern. "Should the major wish to press charges against you and you caught red-handed with the evidence, and you not in uniform . . . well, it could be awkward, wouldn't you say, sergeant?"

With the morning sunlight now streaming through his office window, Calum gave up all hope of seeing his bed. "If you'll excuse me, gentlemen," he said, "I'll just away and feed my prisoners."

"You've got prisoners . . . here?" the sergeant asked, eyeing Calum with ever-awakening interest.

"I'm afraid, with all that's been happening, I clean forgot about them," Calum confessed, shame faced. "They're the poachers who came over on the ferry yesterday. The gillie and I found their car last night, with some fine fish in the boot, so we just waited for them to turn up. They came tearing out of the woods as if all the devils in hell were after them, straight into our arms.

"I expect it was the fright you gave them, sergeant, that set them at the running." Calum nodded in the direction of his typewriter. "I was making a start on the report when you all arrived in on me.

11

Calum the Peacemaker

Constable Calum McKinnon was not outwardly a religious man. He was not to be seen, best suited, shoe polished, with bible tucked under the right arm progressing solemnly of a Sunday morning to church.

This absence of the visible symbols of inner grace did not, however, mean that he was indifferent as to the fate of the immortal soul which, he had no doubt, lurked somewhere within his not inconsiderable frame. Uncommitted, and consequently unhampered by an adherence to either of the two prominent churches established on his island, Calum felt equally at ease in the Rev Roderick McPherson's manse as he did in the chapel house of Father John Galbraith. Thus it was that on the river bank one mild autumn evening the three plied their salmon rods together, at peace with their world.

Leisurely, through the fading light, the tapered cast uncurled across the rock-rippled waters of the stream, the terminal fly alighting as gently as a spent moth on a favoured lie beneath the tree line on the opposite bank. A second's flash of rising silver, a taking swirl, and the fly was gone.

"Play him fine Roddy, a game one by the looks," Father John advised, his voice betraying the controlled excitement of a fellow angler at the moment of the strike.

Downstream, Calum laid aside his rod, extended the handle of his landing-net and waded to the assistance of the Rev McPherson.

When darkness had merged bush and river bank, they sat at their ease, stretching their stockinged feet to the warmth of a blazing fire in the book-lined study of Keldalick manse.

"Well, Roddy," said Father John from the depths of a well-upholstered chair, his forefinger teasing strong, dark tobacco into the scorched bowl of his pipe. "This time next week you'll be on your way to Canada. Man, it's the grand opportunity, but we're going to miss your company."

"Och, it's only for one year. I'll be back before you know it," the minister reasoned. "Anyway, there'll be my exchange partner, the Reverend McCracken. You'll help him settle in and feel at home."

"We'll surely do that," Calum affirmed, passing a lighted taper for Father John's pipe.

Father John was among the reception committee of kirk elders on the pier waiting to welcome off the mainland ferry, the guest minister from Canada. In the crush of passengers disembarking down the gangway they spied a tall young man wearing a dark suit and clerical collar. Weighed in each hand was a heavy leather case, pinned under one arm a lesser travelling bag and, clenched between his teeth, a boat ticket. There was a move to relieve the arrival of his burdens and in response to a look of appeal from the senior elder, Father John stepped forward and introduced the company, leaving himself to the last. "And I am Father John Galbraith of St Ciaran's."

For the space of a moment surprise registered on the

young minister's face. Then, his features broadening into a delighted grin, he seized Father John's extended hand. "I'm sure pleased to meet you, sir."

An impatient clearing of the throat caused him to step hastily to one side. A grey haired man of middle years and similarly attired was revealed.

"I'm afraid there's been a slight misunderstanding," the young minister addressed the company in some embarrassment. "I'm the Reverent Andrew Morrison. This is the Reverend McCracken who has kindly permitted me to accompany him on his visit to your island."

The introductory ceremony was repeated. But in place of the young man's enthusiastic pumping of his hand, Father John was accorded only the briefest acknowledgement by the Rev McCracken before the arrivals turned from him and, flanked by the elders, departed for the manse.

The following morning it was the young minister who opened the manse door and welcomed Father John and an off-duty Constable McKinnon through to the study.

"I hope our visit isn't an inconvenience, and yourselves at the settling in. We thought we'd just look in and see if there was anything we could be doing for you," said Father John.

"That's downright hospitable of you, gentlemen," the young man enthused, flopping into a chair after seeing his visitors comfortably seated. "I've a thousand questions to ask you about the island, the people . . . oh, just about everything."

"We'll be only too pleased . . ." Father John was interrupted by the study door being suddenly thrown open. The Rev McCracken's voice preceded him.

"When I ask you to do something, Andrew, I expect it to be done."

The but lately ordained Andrew Morrison sprang to his

feet at the entrance of his senior. "Father John and Constable McKinnon have called to see if there's anything we need. They were just about to give me a run-down on the parish."

The Rev McCracken continued to address himself to the junior. "I'm obliged to these gentlemen, but they can rest assured that we have all we require."

He paused. Then glancing pointedly at Father John, he continued. "And Andrew, I believe that my thirty years experience in the Kirk has adequately fitted me to administer a parish without the benefit of outside guidance. Now, as there still remains unpacking to be done . . ." The Rev McCracken bestowed on his visitors a smile which held neither humour nor warmth.

Nature had blessed Calum McKinnon with an exceptionally thick skin. The constable rose unruffled from his seat. "The river's fishing well this year," he said. "Perhaps you gentlemen would care to try your hand with me this evening?"

The young minister's eyes lit up at the prospect. His joy was short lived.

"Thank you, Constable, but I fear we'll have little time for amusements," the Rev McCracken's tone left no room for compromise. "We'll both be fully occupied here, doing the Lord's work. I bid you good-morning."

The young man saw them to the door. "I'm really sorry that we can't come with you this evening."

"There'll be other opportunities," Calum commiserated.

"I expect so," replied the young man, but with little conviction.

The mild westerly breezes of autumn gave way to cooler airs from the east and as the evenings gradually shortened, the islanders braced themselves for the winter to some. Divorced as they were from the commercial amusement of the mainland, they had always made their own entertainments to fill the long, dark nights. But strangely, following the arrival of the guest minister, a perceptible and progressive change took place in the tenor of island life. The ceilidhs and dances, held in the large kirk hall, were less and less well attended, and finally abandoned altogether. The popular bingo sessions suffered a like fate, and even the weekly meeting of the whist club, a particular pleasure for Father John and his absent friend the Rev McPherson, held in his own smaller chapel hall, fell by the way when the kirk members ceased to attend and more than half the tables remained unoccupied. It was as though a sickness had smitten the islanders for which they had no immunity.

It was a duffle-coated, concerned Father John who sought out Constable McKinnon at the police station one morning after early mass.

"I'm really disturbed, Calum," Father John admitted. "Our two churches have always got along famously together and there's no man more thought of on the island by my people than the Reverend McPherson. So what in the name of all the saints has happened to us these last few months?"

"Aye, it's the great pity the Reverend McPherson's away in Canada," mourned Calum. "Himself up at the manse is not knowing our ways and maybe not all that anxious to learn, would you say, Father?"

"I've no doubt he's completely sincere in his beliefs, but no, not at all amenable to advice," replied the priest gloomily.

A ponderous silence followed broken only by the ticking of the office clock and the handkerchief-muffled sneezing of Father John.

"A bit of a cold, Father?" enquired Calum.

"Afraid so," wheezed Father John. "This wind cuts right through you."

Oddly enough, this appraisal of the prevailing weather seemed to cheer Calum wonderously. "And bleak December fast ensuing, baith snell an keen," he quoted, perhaps a little uncharitably considering the ailing condition of his visitor. "Och, it's a glass of hot toddy and into bed with yourself," Calum prescribed, seeing Father John to the front door. "And don't you be worrying, I'm thinking that it will all sort itself out and not before long too."

Calum waited till almost closing time before entering the grocer shop in the main street of the village. Apart from the sparse figure behind the counter of the owner, Hector Campbell, who was also the senior kirk elder, the place was empty. Calum hung the cardboard 'Closed' sign on the glass panel of the door and, dropping the snib, turned to the counter. Hector Campbell did not protest his enforced early closing.

"It's yourself, Calum," he said, laying aside his ledger, but avoiding direct eye contact with the arrival's gaze.

"I was thinking we might have a word Hector about . . . this and that," began Calum casually examining the printed ingredients on a tin of soup. "There doesn't seem to be much life about the place these days, maybe you've noticed? Our Canadian guests must be thinking us a very dull lot, wouldn't you say?"

"Ach, you know as well as I do that it's himself up at the manse's doing," exploded Hector, who had no patience for the cat-and-mouse game. "He has it, chapter and verse, that dancing and card-playing . . . *a dhia*, anything that's fun at all, is desperate sinful. The man's hell-bent on saving us all from Eternal Damnation!"

"Eternal Damnation you say Hector," Calum's bushed

eyebrows raised. "*Mo creach*, that's not something to be contemplated lightly. But I'm believing that the Reverend McPherson would have taken that into consideration before allowing the ceilidhs in the kirk hall all these years. So I'm fairly confident that our souls are in no great jeopardy."

"There's not a one of us had any doubts on that score, man. But yon minister will only be here for a wee while so we don't want to fall out with him and maybe grieve his own Reverence when he comes home. I can't see anything for it but just to go along with him for the present and hope that things will get back to normal when he leaves."

"Black shame on you Hector," Calum chided, "to give up so easily, and you every bit as fly a Campbell as the old fox himself in his lair at Inveraray."

"It's not a matter of outwitting him, Calum," Hector explained sadly. "He's what the past has made him. You see, at the time of the Clearances whole congregations went out to Canada with their minister leading them. The Old Testament was their law and the reformed church their ideal. It was a hard struggle just to survive and the very strength of the faith which sustained them made them intolerant of other peoples' beliefs and customs. A man like that can't change overnight."

"I see what you mean, Hector," said Calum, chastened. "Mind you, the young minister's not like that, so perhaps there's hope yet . . . eh, Hector? It seems to me," continued Calum after a bit of thought, "that what we need is a public event which would involve everybody on the island. That might break the ice."

"Aye, but what?" puzzled Hector.

"I have it," announced Calum, "Remembrance Sunday is next week. We could have a combined service at the War Memorial, that should do the trick. I'll take a turn round tomorrow and put it to him."

The following day at the manse Calum apologised for Father John's absence on account of his ill health. Then implying that he spoke—as indeed he did—for the islanders as a whole, he outlined the proposal for a combined service.

"I have no desire to appear offensive, Constable McKinnon," declared the Rev McCracken, "but I would have you know that the Kirk can stand on its own feet without extraneous support. I would deny no man, no matter how misguided he might be, the freedom to worship as his conscience dictates. But on a matter of principle, I will not compromise. A combined service is out of the question."

On the doorstep the young minister looked dolefully at Calum. "He'll not give an inch, you know."

"As I recall," mused Calum, "he said he would deny no man the right to worship according to conscience. Am I right?"

"Yes, and he meant it," confirmed the young man.

"I'm counting on that," declared Calum as he strode off purposefully in the direction of a ramshackle garage at the head of the pier.

In the vestuary of the kirk, the Rev McCracken shivered in his black gown as the organ anthem heralded his entrance. The people rose for the opening hymn and as their voices filled the church he observed from the vantage of the pulpit that the entire congregation was woollen-gloved and mufflered. The building was as cold as charity.

The service over, Hector Campbell knocked at the vestuary door and entered with the collection plate. Teeth clenched against their chattering, the minister fumbled with numbed fingers at the buttons of his overcoat.

"A fine sermon, Minister," Hector congratulated. "The

wages of sin and the fires of Hell. Och, I'm thinking that you got through to a few of them this morning."

"The heating would have benefited from a few embers of that fire today," the Rev McCracken suggested, his lips already quite blue with the chilled air. "What has happened?"

"The heating?" Hector echoed as if the word was new to his vocabulary. "Ach, was it not myself that clean forgot to tell you that it would be off . . . on account of this being Ramadan, you'll understand."

"Ramadan?"

"Just that, Minister," said Hector piously. "And Kushi at the fasting and praying from dawn to dusk."

"Kushi?"

"Kushi Mohamed . . . the boilerman. A rare hand he is to be sure with that old heap of rusting iron," praised the elder.

"Are you seriously telling me that the boilerman is a . . . is a . . ." The unacceptable defying expression, the minister's unfinished sentence hung in the air as the glow of a rising flush on his cheeks suggested that the chilliness of the room had ceased to be his prime concern.

"A Moslem, aye Minister, the genuine article," assured Hector. "Kushi was stationed here during the war, and with the grand understanding he was having with engines and the likes, did we not persuade him to stay to and run the garage at the pier? He does the boiler, as a sort of favour, and doesn't charge us a penny." As speech appeared to be beyond the minister, Hector suggested sensibly. "If you keep your coat on and maybe wear an extra pullover, you'll hardly feel the cold."

December came in a flurry of hail and snow and with the approach of Christmas, Calum judged that Allah had had a pretty fair crack of the whip, considering that He only had one, and prior to Calum's visit to the garage, lapsed adherent on the island. On the first Suday of the month the Rev McCracken was able to mount the steps to the pulpit, unhampered by extra winter clothing.

The expectation was that with the thawing out of the preacher's pulpit would come a mellowing of his concept of the brotherhood of man. It was not to be realised. It was during a chance encounter one evening that Calum learned from the young minister an intellegence which paled the Rev McCracken's previous assaults on the island's institutions into insignificance.

"The Christmas bazaar's to be held on Saturday and as he's fully occupied with other matters, he's instructed me to make all the arrangemants," the young man reported.

"But doesn't he realise that the bazaar is the big event of the season for us. Everyone on the island gets involved," protested Calum.

"I know that the elders did try to get that across to him, but he's decided that it's solely a kirk affair, and that's that."

His many years of dealing with impossible people and lunatic situations stood Calum in good stead at that moment for, within him, he felt the sensations of mounting anger. They walked on in silence for some time. Then, in a tone that had the measured quality of a mathematician summarising the elements of a calculation, he said. "He definitely specified that it should be on Saturday, am I right? And that you are to attend to all the arrangements?"

"Yes," replied his companion without enthusiasm.

"Then he's not likey to interfere till he arrives to open the proceedings?"

"I should think it most unlikely," was the confirmation.

"Then, go you ahead and make the arrangemants. The elders and Father John's people will give you all the assistance you need," instructed Calum. The look of bewilderment that was directed at him caused a smile to ghost on the genial McKinnon features. "The Lord, as I'm sure I don't have to remind you, sir, works in mysterious ways His wonders to perform."

Saturday dawned fine with no suggestion of wind or rain. A steady stream of islanders took the road bearing heavy baskets and packages. At the hall all was bustle and activity; the walls draped with gay bunting and tinsel hung on the Christmas tree. The baking was priced and displayed; the wheel-of-fortune tested, darts in the twenty, 3 balls in the bucket set up, anything which would show a profit and provide entertainment was made ready. As morning gave way to afternoon, from all corners of the island they came; by car and tractor, by bicycle and on foot, dressed in their Sunday best. The commencement hour of 2pm was not far distant.

At the manse an edgy young minister reminded the Rev McCracken that it was time to be on their way.

"Don't fuss, Andrew," the senior rebuked, gathering up the notes of his prepared speech. "Start the car and I'll be right with you."

With his passenger finally aboard, the young man drove to the crossroads at the foot of Manse Brae and, turning to the right, accelerated down the road.

"What are you thinking of," the passenger protested, "you should have gone left for the church hall."

The driver's hands tightened on the steering wheel while he drew a deep breath. "I know, sir, but you see I've had to change the venue."

"You've had to do what?" came the startled response.

"I suppose I could have insisted on the hall being opened

but, knowing your strict views on not doing unnecessary work on the Sabbath, I . . ."

"In the name of sanity, Andrew, what are you talking about? Today is Saturday," reasoned the older man.

The palms of the unfortunate young man were slippery with sweat. "I know, sir, but if you'll recollect, it's also the Jewish Sabbath."

"But we're not Jews, Andrew," the Rev McCracken's endurance was reaching its limit as he twisted round to stare unblinking at his associate.

"No . . . but our hall-keeper, Sammy Goldstein is," came the dry mouthed reply.

The car swung in to the grounds of St Cirian's and drew to a halt before the chapel hall. A tumultuous welcome greeted the Rev McCracken as he was assisted from the car by Father John and led through the throng to the holly bedecked platform. An arm firmly hooked through that of the guest of honour, the priest addressed the crowd.

"Friends, may I say what pleasure it gives me to welcome to St Cirian's our respected visitor from Canada and how happy we all are that he has consented to open our Christmas bazaar." Father John had to wait for the prolonged applause to subside before concluding. "Ladies and gentlemen, friends . . . the Reverend McCracken."

To the expectant faces before him the Rev McCracken betrayed nothing of the outrage which he felt. With what high hopes he had sailed to preach the Word in the very birthplace of the Kirk only to find himself totally at the mercy of Mosque and Synagogue. And now, lauded and feted in the camp of the Idolaters. Had the world gone mad?

"Never, in all my life," he resounded, nostrils flared, "have I been so . . ." he was about to say insulted when he identified among the faces of his audience the majority of his congregation and all of his elders, completely at home in their surroundings . . . "delighted and er . . . proud than I am to be here among you today . . ."

The evening of the Rev McPherson's return from Canada found him and his two old friends, Father John and Constable McKinnon, seated before a crackling fire in the study of the manse.

"Well now," said the Rev McPherson, "I know that you're both anxious to hear all about my time in Canada. But first, tell me, how were things here? No problems I hope, nothing I should be knowing about?"

"Everything went just grand," Calum answered blandly, "more or less."

12

A Thorn In The Flesh

Calum decided that with a full moon on the rise, the fresh run sea-trout in the pool had become too wary of the light and his every movement. Reluctantly he wound in his line, hooked the tail fly to the cork handle of his old cane rod and consoled by the weight of one good fish in his bag, he stepped out on the half mile walk back to his home.

Home for Constable Calum McKinnon was a 1930s bungalow with an office attached where comfortably distanced from the constraints of the mainland, he maintained the Queen's peace alone and in a manner individual to himself. There were few houses on the island where he was not welcomed.

He had gone barely half the way when the sounds of muted laughter told him that he was not the only one abroad that night. Laying down his fish tackle he approached the stone dyke separating him from the source of the merriment.

Cautiously, Calum raised his head above the level of the wall which enclosed the cottage and bit of garden of Mrs McLean, a widow in her late seventies and severely deaf. Below, their backs towards him, he observed and identified two young men who were uprooting the widow's leeks and carrots with spirited abandon and tossing them into the air.

Demonstrating an agility surprising for a man of his bulk, Calum was over the wall and with a reveller grasped firmly by the scruff of the neck in each hand, he headed for the widow's rain-barrel close by her potting shed. With the easy rhythm of a piston-engine, Calum alternated the plunging and raising of their heads in the green-slimed water of the barrel until by the lessening of his captives struggles, he judged that they would be amenable to a suggestion he had in mind as to how they might occupy the remainder of the night.

On release, the two slid retching and gasping to the ground.

"Well bless me, if it isn't young Ronald from the hotel, and Hector Campbell of Ballymeanach's boy, Ian," Calum declared with all the warmth of a long lost uncle. "*A dhia*, but it's proud I am to be finding that two young gentlemen like yourselves, studying hard at university, should be spending their well earned holidays tending an old lady's garden." Calum's tone took on the properties of a benediction as he added. "And in the middle of the night too, so that herself would be thinking it was the little people who had done her the kindness."

The absence of any reponse from the bedraggled pair at his feet Calum put down to their understandable embarrassment at being discovered performing an act of charity. "Och, but I'm interrupting you with my blethers," he apologised, leaning his back against the rain-barrel and pulling out his tobacco-pouch.

"I'll just have a few draws at my pipe while you get on with the replanting." He cast a sorrowful eye round the garden. "It's not much that the Old One can be doing nowadays, so

I've no doubt when you've finished her vegetables you'll be giving her flower beds a bit of weeding, and after that there'll be the . . ."

A week to the very day following the garden episode, Calum was in his office going through the mail just arrived with the steamer. Among the usual amendments and gazettes was a letter bearing his name, rank and number. Calum opened the envelope and gingerly extracted a memorandum signed, he was quick to ascertain, by no less a person than his Inspector on the mainland. As it was not the wont of his gallant leader to address him personally, unless there were matters of a doomsday nature to be communicated, Calum nerved himself for what was to come.

It appeared that the Inspector had received a letter from the Convener of the Island's Council expressing the dissatisfaction of that august body with Calum's method of policing. In the Council's view he spent too much time cruising about in a taxpayer-funded patrol car and not enough footing it along the highways and byways where, Calum was amazed to learn, vandals and malcontents abounded.

He was instructed that as from the moment of receipt, foot-patrols were to be the order of the day with a written report detailing all such duties to be submitted daily and that for an indefinite period. The inspector advised that he would be keeping a sharp eye on Calum's subsequent performance, and that any backsliding on his part would be dealt with.

Placing the memorandum on the desk before him, Calum leaned back in his chair and reflected that for more than a quarter of a century he had been receiving similar instructions from his superiors on the mainland.

The reasoning behind such orders had always been a puzzle to him but, assuming that they were founded on some proven theory that the best qualified to know how to police an island was he who never set foot on one, he had reconciled himself to their execution. However there were times like the present when he found himself questioning that assumption.

In the days that followed Calum was inundated by offers of lifts and cups of tea to revive and sustain him as he trudged the dusty roads of his island. It was common knowledge that Lachie Mor the Ambulance was on standby to run him to the Cottage Hospital the moment his stride should falter.

That the telephone might be bouncing off his office desk or the patrol car wireless hoarse calling for him was seemingly to be of little consequence. That he should do the will of his masters was all that was required. Back at the station Calum's wife, Jean answered the incoming calls in his absence with the information that, "Acting on the Inspector's instructions, himself is at the walking and only the Lord knows where he might be." A decent woman, raised in a Christian home, poor Jean could only close her ears to the profane indignities wished on all the inspectors when the callers found themselves denied immediate access to the ear of their constable.

Truth to tell, after years of being at the beck and call of those twin wonders of modern communication, Calum was rather enjoying his new won freedom.

In spite of his lady wife's encouragement that the exercise would do his expanding waistline the world of good, Calum was still finding the hills something of a trial when, labouring up Pier Road one morning, he came upon the two young students with a bent for late night horticulture, Ronald and Ian.

"A grand day for a wee stroll, Constable," Ronald called to him.

"But a bit hard on the bunions, maybe," Ian grinned.

Speech being beyond Calum through lack of breath, he had to content himself with pausing in his stride and eyeing the humorous twosome seated on a low wall idly swinging their legs.

"I expect you must be grateful to the Council for getting you out of that nasty old car and back into the fresh air again," Ronald suggested, stuggling to keep a straight face. Wisely in the circumstances, the young men recognised the deepening of the flush on Calum's cheeks as an outward sign of emotional rather than physical stress. Easing themselves off the wall they began a strategic retreat with just one parting sally from the irrepressible Ronald. "I'll be sure to mention to my father how well you're doing as a foot-slogger, Constable McKinnon."

The weakness of the ultra-smart has always been that they never know when to quit and young Ronald had been no exception. As Calum applied himself once more to the gradient of the hill, he had much to occupy his thoughts. From the outset he had found it odd, knowing the islanders as he did, that the idea of his wandering around and poking his nose too closely into their affairs could possibly have been the will of the community as expressed through their council. Seemingly, he had become the target for certain disaffected persons operating from positions of influence. The foot-patrols could well be only a sighting shot across his bows, the prelude to a broadside of impossible restrictions on his freedom of action.

There was a look of surprise in the eyes of the dapper little man who opened the front door of his neatly appointed bungalow to Calum's knock. The stress of a working life behind the counter of a Glasgow bank behind him, Mr Fraser had but lately retired to the island to find peace of mind along its shores and craggy hills, bird-watching. Flattered by the ready acceptance of the islanders, he'd been easily persuaded to take over the duties of secretary to the Council.

Awkwardly abalancing an excessively fine teacup on his knee in the lounge of the bungalow, Calum chatted about this and that, as is the island way, before coming to the point of his visit.

"I've just been to the village hall," he mentioned, "but there was no sign of the minutes of the last Council meeting on the notice board."

"Oh," Mr Fraser exclaimed, the stomach cramps he'd experienced in his bank days with each new crisis reasserting themselves. "I typed them myself and passed them to the Convener for his approval. I simply can't think why he hasn't posted them by this time." Mr Fraser seemed genuinely distressed and the cramps worsening if anything.

"Och, don't be upsetting yourself now, Mr Fraser," Calum soothed. "I expect that it's having his son Ronald home from the university that's put it clean out of his mind. But you'll have a copy by you, I've no doubt, that maybe I could be having a wee look at?"

Calum quickly scanned the copy of the minutes, readily supplied by Mr Fraser, until he found the item concerning police foot-patrols. Proposed, he saw, by the Convener, seconded by the Vice-Converner, and passed unanimously. He handed back the sheet and, to Mr Fraser's relief, rose to leave.

"It was a right wet night when the meeting was held, as I remember," Calum remarked innocently. "There wouldn't be many of the . . ." he gave Mr Fraser a we-incomers-should-stick-together wink " . . .locals there, I shouldn't think?"

Mr Fraser, calmed both in mind and stomach by Calum's own implied inclusion in the island's immigrant society, vigorously nodded his agreement.

"Not one, apart from the Converner and Vice-Convener of course. There were barely enough of us to constitute a quorum.

"*Mo creach*, do you tell me that now?" Calum commiserated, putting on his cap. "Just no sense of responsibility at all, these islanders," he deplored. "Where in the wide world would they be, I wonder, without a helping hand from the likes of yourself, Mr Fraser?"

The Saturday of the sheep sales ranked almost with Christmas on the island's festival calendar. Ruddy faced farmers, with equally healthy wallets, poured off the early morning steamer to throng the auction mart. The objects of their interest, close penned around the sale ring, were studied, discussed, prodded with crooks and evaluated, fleece, horn and hoof, to the last penny.

As the day wore on and the pens emptied, business in the hotel bar took a decided upward turn till, by early evening, it was standing room only with just the fittest winning their way to the counter. When the mainlanders had finally departed on the late boat, the islanders continued to debate the gains or losses of the day over a last dram, before drifting off homewards in ones and twos by moonlight.

Deep in the shadow of a doorway opposite the hotel, Calum nudged his companion. Stealthily the two crossed the road to press themselves flat against the wall of the hotel. Removing his cap, Calum stretched up to peer through the lit window of the bar, then ducked back down again. Motioning his companion to follow him, he stepped swiftly to the entrance and pressing his ear against the door, he held his breath to listen. At the sound of the till ringing up a sale he contained himself for the count of three then, easing open the door he was into the room with his companion close at his heels, then across to the counter just as the owner was in the act of handing over to a customer the change of a ten pound note.

"I'll take charge of that," Calum declared, his paw-like hand emcompassing the proffered notes. "Evidence, you'll understand," he offered by way of explanation. Eyeing the amber filled glass on the counter before the startled customer, he enquired of his companion, Special Constable Douglas McDonald. "What, Dougie, would you be thinking might be in that glass?"

Dougie's brows creased in puzzlement. "Well now," he ventured, "it has the looks of whisky." He lifted the glass and sniffed at the contents. "Aye, and the smell too," he opinioned, before raising it to his mouth. "Not the shadow of a doubt," he affirmed, smacking his lips, "as fine a malt as I've tasted ever."

In a tone in keeping with solemnity of the proceedings, Calum cautioned and charged the dumbfounded hotel-keeper with an offence, hitherto unheard of on the island, of selling or supplying *Uisge-Beatha* outwith the permitted hours. The full significance of the hotelier's reply to the charge, which Calum dutifully recorded in his notebook, would have been lost on all but native speakers of the gaelic tongue.

While Calum's head was bent over his notebook, the bar's deprived customer muttered a hurried, "I'd better be getting back to Ballymeanach," as he made for the door.

"A moment of your time, Mr Campbell," Calum stopped him in his tracks without so much as looking up from his writing. "As a witness for the prosecution in this case, I'll be requiring a statement from you." Then raising his head he added, "And of course, there's the charges against yourself to be considered."

"What charges?" Mr Campbell demanded to know. "If

I'm to be a witness I can't be charged too . . . surely?"

"Och no, that would not be proper at all," Calum confirmed. "It's the expired excise licence and the bald front tyre on the landrover parked outside I was referring to. It is yours, is it not?"

The telephone call from his Inspector the following morning did not come altogether as a surprise to Calum.

"You were lucky to catch me in, Inspector," he congratulated. "I was just about to foot patrol to Ach-an-Droma where I've heard tell of a faulty silencer on that old car belonging to Roddy McLeod, him that's maried to the cousin of . . ."

"Quite, quite," the Inspector interrupted Calum's geneological flow, "it's about that I wanted to speak to you."

"A dhia," Calum was impressed, "so you've heard over there on the mainland about Roddy's silencer?"

"Of course not, man," the Inspector was controlling himself, but with difficulty. "I've been giving the matter of your foot-patrols further consideration and feel that having you out of communication for prolonged periods is counter productive."

"Och I'm not sure that you're right there, sir," Calum dared to object. "Now that you've put me back on my feet it's myself that's been producing away like anything. Why, only last night . . ."

"Ah . . . yes, McKinnon," the Inspector was conciliatory. "I was coming to that. I've received a most apologetic telephone call from the owner of the Clachan Hotel. He deeply regrets the unfortunate incident in his bar last night, when he inadvertantly served a customer after hours. It appears that his clock had stopped and he hadn't noticed."

"There was no mention of clocks in his reply to the charge, Inspector," Calum replied doubtfully, flicking through the pages of his notebook.

"An oversight, McKinnon," the Inspector snapped, before forcing himself back to sweet reasonableness. "A prominent member of the community, of blameless character, understandable in the circumstances that he should be . . . em . . . confused."

Calum recalled little confusion in the hotelier's lucid, indeed eloquent condemnation of the country's addle-brained licensing laws and the mindless cretins who enforced them. However, he deemed it prudent to remain silent.

"I don't expect you've put anything down on paper yet." There was a quality of menace in the Inspector's expectation which suggested to his listener that a negative reply was being sought.

"Haven't really had time, sir," Calum confessed, "but I'll get down to it the moment I get back from Ach-an-Droma."

"Naturally the decision is entirely up to you, McKinnon," the Inspector advised. "But considering the hotelier's flawless record and his position as Convener to the Council, a prosecution against him for an offence which is, I'm sure you'll agree, more of a technical than criminal nature, could well damage the fine reputation of the Council as a whole which would be most regrettable. In this instance, purely from a public relations point of view you'll understand, McKinnon, perhaps a sharp warning from yourself might suffice."

"Well, sir," said Calum, as though giving the matter deep thought, "what you suggest might be best in the long run . . . for all concerned, as it were."

"Good," replied the Inspector. "I'll leave it to you then. Keep me informed."

"Indeed I will," promised Calum. "And about the foot-patrols, sir you were saying earlier . . ."

"Just exercise your own judgement, McKinnon," the Inspector instructed about to replace the receiver.

"And about the other charges, Inspector?" Calum persisted.

"What other charges?" the Inspector enquired.

"The expired licence and bald tyre on the Vice-Convener's Landrover," Calum explained.

"Oh, those," the Inspector answered with diminished interest, his mind already withdrawing from the concerns of a peripheral province of his considerable empire. "Yes, by all means submit a report, there's far too much of that kind of thing going on nowadays."

"Right you are, sir," Calum agreed, "and I'll be at the warning of the Convener this very day." Then, as if in afterthought he added, "Would there be any messages, of a personal nature you'd like me to be giving him while I'm there . . . him being your brother-in-law and all?"

13

Calum's Guiding Hand

"You'll have him for a week, Calum." There was a note of commiseration in Sergeant Carmichael's voice. Ages with Calum McKinnon and his accomplice in many a fine ploy when they'd lodged together as young recruits, he felt as Brutus must have when he plunged the dagger into his old friend Ceasar. "The inspector sees him as the Great White Hope of the division, oozing leadership potential."

At the end of the phone in his tiny island police office, Calum washed down that piece of information with the day's first cup of strong coffee.

"But why send him here?" Calum reasonably enquired,

Great White Hopes being the rarest of birds on his island.

"The inspector reckons that a bit of overseas duty will look good on his record . . . shows initiative, works well on his own, requires the minimum supervision, you know the patter, Calum," the sergeant replied. All the aforementioned qualities appeared in Calum's own personal record but, as the inspector never tired of telling him, in the negative column.

"He'll be arriving on the morning ferry," the sergeant advised, "and Calum, maybe I should mention that he's . . . eh,"

"Yes, Sergeant," Calum encouraged, "He's what?"

"The inspector's daughter's current boyfriend."

The division's wonder boy was not difficult to identify, coming down the gangway of the boat. Tall, if by island standards skinny, his neatly trimmed hair, erect bearing and decisive chin marked him clearly as a man of destiny.

"Welcome to the island, Dick," Calum greeted, offering his hand.

"Richard," the young man corrected. "I prefer to be addressed by my proper name," he advised, transferring his travelling bag to his host's outstretched hand. Withdrawing from his pocket a buff coloured envelope, he then added. "This contains your instructions from the inspector. I suggest that you read them . . . now."

With the deference due to a document from so august a personage as the inspector, Calum eased open the envelope and scanned the contents. From the warmth of the communication, he suspected that it had been kept overnight in the refrigerator. Unsuitable as he was, the inspector stated, to act as mentor to so promising a constable as Richard Havelock-Smythe, he was however to place himself completely at the disposal of that young man and offer him all possible opportunities to benefit from his sojourn on the the island.

Calum's responsibility was to be little more than a guide. The numerous prosecutions, which would undoubtably result from the visit, would be handled by Havelock-Smythe, with Calum's role merely that of a witness.

Calum looked up from the paper to find that his charge had already installed himself in the driving seat of Calum's patrol car and was drumming his fingers impatiently on the driving wheel. Surprised but not put out by this presumption, Calum loaded the bag into the boot of the car and, taking his place in the unaccustomed front passenger seat, he directed a course to the house of the widow McLeod where he'd booked the arrival in for a week.

Leaving Havelock-Smythe to settle in, Calum returned to his office satisfied that he had left his charge in the best possible hands. Mrs McLeod's two unmarried and, for the eligible bachelors on the island, over anxious daughters, would certainly do all in their power to make the stranger's stay a memorable one.

Calum had barely glanced at the headlines of the daily paper when Havelock-Smythe arrived business-like in his office.

"That public-house down the road, the Tigh a' Chlachain needs a bit of watching," he announced, his eye running distastefully round the incumbent's not over tidy office. "The doors were open one minute and forty seconds before the proper time. I checked it on my watch."

"As much as that?" Calum registered surprise bordering on disbelief.

The rest of that morning and the afternoon proved to be one of the longest Calum could recall. The young man was a power-house of energy. An area of land which, weather permitting, would take Calum a leisurely week to cover, was rocketed over in a couple of hours. And this included numerous halts to measure tyre treads and the braking efficiency of little boys' bicycles.

Happily for Calum, the nearest he got to fulfilling his alloted role as witness was when he was jerked out of the gloomiest of meditations by the patrol car shuddering to a halt opposite the cottage of Old Angus the Cobbler. Before Calum could reach for the door handle, the young bloodhound was half way up the garden path. By the time Calum caught up with him his notebook was out and name, age and occupation being demanded.

"*Co e an t-amadan a tha so, a Chaluim?*" The old man asked Calum who the idiot was in his native Gaelic.

"Is he foreign?" Havelock-Smythe enquired, somewhat taken aback.

A policeman on a Gaelic speaking island who didn't recognise the language when he heard it was, Calum considered, hardly in a position to talk about foreigners.

"Born here, as his father was, and his father before him," Calum replied. "Och, he understands English just fine, but considers its use only good enough for women and children . . ." Calums eyes surveyed the garden before coming to rest on the puzzled face of Havelock-Smythe, " . . . and the likes," he concluded.

Sensing that he was losing command of the situation, Havelock-Smythe blurted out. "He was watering his potatoes from that blue tub there and as I explained to him when I cautioned him, that is contrary to the restrictions on the use of water during this drought." The pencil poised, ready for action. "Was what he said in reply to the charge?"

"Not quite," said Calum evasively. A brief exchange took

place between him and the ancient Gael, which ended with much laughing and back-slapping as Calum turned away and headed for the gate.

"But what about my charge?" Havelock-Smythe called after him.

"It was his daughter's baby's bath water. I'm not thinking that the Fiscal would be all that interested," informed Calum over his shoulder as he climbed into the car.

In the late evening they were heading back for the office and Calum was having pleasant thoughts of supper. Of a sudden the patrol car accelerated, the siren wailing, in hot pursuit of a small blue Ford car.

"I've been observing that driver. He gave a hand signal as well as using his flashers when he overtook that tractor. Too perfect driving is a sure sign of a drunk driver," his all of 18 months service standing Havelock-Smythe in good stead.

By the light of his torch, the young officer studied the man at the wheel of the blue Ford—black Homburg hat and top-coat, his somewhat austere features partially obscured by the many folds of a white scarf. A business man on his way home after an expense-account dinner, the young sleuth deduced and made the statutory requirement for a breath sample.

Calum, mindful of the role allotted to him in the inspector's communication, stationed himself just outside the circle of lamp light and witnessed away like mad. Never a one to grudge praise where praise is due, he could not but admire the composure of his young companion in the face of the storm of abuse directed at him from the interior of the the blue Ford. Acknowledgement was also due to the abuser for, without once descending to common obscenities, he consigned, lock, stock and barrel, whole generations of Havelock-Smythes to the eternal fires of Hades. Fortunately, as the transfer was conducted in Gaelic, the consignor remained mercifuly unaware of his proposed future posting.

The plastic bag, Calum observed, went back and forward, uninflated, through the window of the car like a ball in a tennis court. Finally, the young constable deciding that his requirement had met with a refusal, hauled the driver from his car and, in a litany of cautioning and charging, frog-marched him to the police patrol car.

"I'll take the prisoner. You bring in his car," he fired off at Calum, and drove off.

Conscious of the responsibility of being in charge of another's vehicle, Calum progressed sedately towards the police station, stopping en route at the doctor's house to uplift him. A friend of long standing, Calum knew that it was the good doctor's habit to take a wee dram or two before retiring to bed, soley as an adjunct to a sound night's sleep, of course.

On arrival at the police station, Calum allowed the doctor to proceed him into the office, while he resumed his onerous duty of witnessing from behind a tall filing cabinet sited near the door.

The first indication that Havelock-Smythe had felt that perhaps he'd been a mite precipitous in effecting an arrest, was when the Homburg-hatted prisoner shed his scarf to reveal a clerical collar of unblemished whiteness. The second was when the doctor hurriedly extracted from his medical bag a piece of apparatus and clamped the terminal mask over the mouth and nose of his prisoner with the injunction to, "Breath slowly and deeply."

While the resuscitation was being performed, Calum saw fit to emerge from behind the cabinet and to confide to the ashen-faced apprehending officer.

"It's a martyr, is his Reverence, to the asthma, especially when he gets excited. *A dhia*, I've seen him addressing meetings of our Temperance Society; being the Free Kirk minister he is of course the president and getting so inflamed at the evils of strong drink that he's had to be put to bed for a week to get his breath back. Come to think of it, this being Monday, he'd have been on his way back to the manse after just such a meeting when you had the eye of him."

Ever the soul of generosity, Calum assured the now freely perspiring Havelock-Smythe that once the reverend gentleman was sufficiently recovered, he'd see him safely home and try to persuade him not to complain of this treatment to the inspector.

It would be, Calum reflected, regrettable, if the force should lose such a valuable asset as Havelock-Smythe at so early a period in his career. "Now, away with you to bed and get a good night's sleep, for we're off at the crack of dawn to the sheep-dipping."

It was a bright morning, with a light breeze clearing the early mist from the hills when they left the patrol car at the roadside and tramped the heather moor to the sheep fank at Ach na Cloiche farm. Clad in his mud-stained Diseases of Animals oilskin and worn wellington boots, Calum cut a poor figure beside the immaculately uniformed Havelock-Smythe, who had declined Calum's offer of old gear, presumably on the principle that a police officer should appear a police officer at all times.

The introduction by Calum of his colleague to Seoras Mor the shepherd and his three burly sons over, the day's work of dippng the flock began. Mustered into holding pens by the dogs, each sheep was dragged by the horns, struggling, to be dropped, without ceremony, into a sunken concrete trough filled with a foul smelling concoction of water and disinfectant. Once in, the sheep was totally submerged by Seoras Mor, standing straddled across the trough, thrusting it under with a long handled brush. The baptism over, the sheep emerged, sodden-fleeced and gasping for air, to scramble as best it could, up the sloping far end.

"Stop." Havelock-Smythe's command rang out, as he looked up from his watch. "Twenty seconds exactly, and the Order requires a minimum of one minute.

The absurdity of the young constable's objection was matched only by the Order itself. In some recess, deep in the heart of the Ministry, red-taped from reality, a 9am to 5pm bureaucrat, whose ability to identify a sheep was likely gleaned while flicking through the pages of Country Life in his dentist's waiting room, had decreed that the luckless animals should spend no less than one minute by the clock, battling for survival. As few, if any, dips in the Scottish Highlands were designed for so long an occupation, a reasonable compromise had to be allowed to avoid the annihilation of the species by drowning.

Calum was about to launch into an explanation of the practicalities of the business when he had a change of mind. After exchanging a swift but meaningful look with the shepherd, he turned to the watch-in-hand young expert.

"I'm not thinking that Seoras Mor is understanding these regulations, not how they should be carried out. Maybe you'd like to be showing him."

No leader worth his salt should ask his men to do what he's not prepared to do himself and as Havelock-Smythe's sights were set on a certain desk in a certain office in far-off Pitt Street, Glasgow, he seized the brush and straddled the trough. His watch well to the fore, Calum stood by and at a nod from him, a sheep was dropped into the water. The moment its head broke the surface, Havelock-Smythe had it under again with a well directed push with the brush.

And so the action continued—head up, push down. For perhaps 40 endless seconds the sheep permitted the indignity to continue, before it struck back. Thrusting off the bottom with both hind legs, it shot upwards, emerging from the murky waters with all the menace of a Polaris missile.

Taken unawares by the sudden eruption of the demented creature, its tormentor took a step backwards and missed his footing on the edge of the trough. Those who have had the experience, claim that men and porpoises play happily together in the enclosure of a pool. The same cannot be said of sheep.

Dutifully, Calum noted the time of Havelock-Smythe's entry into the trough and his eventual rescue from it. The period ammounted to one minute, ten and one half seconds. Without fear of contradiciton, Richard Havelock-Smythe could be declared, above and beyond the letter of the Order, fully protected against Sheep Scab.

There was no question of his travelling back in the patrol car for the stench of his saturated uniform was such that even the dogs slunk off with tails between their legs. The worst of the slime was hosed off him at the fank, after which he was returned to his lodgings by the shepherd in an open trailer coupled to the back of a tractor.

Calum's earlier conviction that his chioce of the house of Mrs McLeod and her two formidable daughters as being suitable lodgings for his young visitor, was fully justified by the sympathy and compassion they bestowed on that unhappy young man as they assisted him from the trailer and up to his bedroom, with not a word of complaint about the pools of muddy water he left in his wake.

Oddly, as they stood on the pier together on the day of departure for his young colleague, Calum felt a sense of loss. Whether it had been the ducking, or perhaps the mothering he'd received at the hands of the McLeod ladies, it's hard to say. But from then onwards their relationship couldn't have been better. Havelock-Smythe kept his notebook where Calum kept his, firmly buttoned away in the breast pocket of his uniform tunic, seeing the light of day only as a last resort. Together they had fished the river and sunk a pint or two and had upheld the Queen's laws, but with a reasonableness which the islanders respected.

"Well Calum, it's goodbye for the present and thanks for all you've done for me," the young man said warmly, as they clasped hands at the foot of the gangway.

"The very best of luck, Dick . . . er, Richard," Calum corrected.

"Dick will do just fine," Havelock-Smythe grinned. "We left Richard back there in the sheep-dip."

14

Jamie

The last stragglers were just clearing the ferry-boat gangway, as Constable Calum McKinnon, anxiously scanning the faces, hurried on to the pier. Crofters returning from the mainland sales, merchant seamen home on leave and salesmen, most known to him by sight and name, pressed past him.

"The new Superintendent will arrive on the Friday ferry," the Inspector had telephoned. "You will be timeously on the pier in best uniform to meet him. Do you understand, McKinnon?" Like a prophet of doom on the eve of the apocalypse he had continued, "The Superintendent who's visiting your island is one of those accelerated promotion whizz-kids, so you won't pull the wool over his eyes. One glance at your pathetic case returns and he'll have you back here in Oban pulling padlocks under my personal supervision."

Calum sighed in resignation as he pictured himself, not for the first time, on the carpet before his superior's desk at the Sub-Divisonal office.

"Constable McKinnon?" a precise authoritative voice enquired at his shoulder. Turning quickly he saw a tall quietly dressed young man with a neatly trimmed moustach. "I believe you are expecting me."

Calum drew himself up and raised his arm awkwardly in an unaccustomed salute.

"I trust you had an easy crossing sir," he managed. "She can be pretty rough when the mood's on her."

"I've known worse," the Superintendent replied absently, his eyes travelling slowly round the rocky bay.

"The Panda car is parked at the head of the quay," Calum informed him, adding without enthusiasm, "the Police Station is only a short drive."

The arrival seemed not to hear him, his gaze moving from the shore to the modest white-washed cottages, then to mountains rising beyond. Calum watched him, perplexed as to what to do or say.

"I could do with some exercise," the Superintendent announced suddenly and set off striding up the quay. "Come Constable, we'll walk."

Just as they were leaving the pier an ancient Austin van wheezed slowly past. With a sinking heart Calum noticed that there was still no trace of an Excise Licence on the front windscreen. He'd told old Duncan Lorrie only last week that he would have to get a new one but he knew old Duncan had no head for paperwork. Didn't Kirsty his wife attend to all that and hadn't she been ill for the past month. Surely the 'whizz-kid' wouldn't have missed such a glaring offence. He cast a quick, guilty glance at his Superintendent's face. The man's features betrayed nothing.

In silence they reached the main street of the village. Those they met gave Calum a nod of the head, their eyes resting curiously for a second in the passing on the stanger.

Outside the Clachan, the village pub, the Superintendent stopped and extracted a cigarette from a gold case.

"One of the benefits of being in plain clothes," he remarked lighting the cigarette from an engraved lighter. Slowly and apparently pleasurably he exhaled a thin column of blue smoke. "I expect," he said meditatively, "being so far from the mainland and the ferry storm bound from time to time, mail deliveries must be rather irregular."

"Well sir," protested Calum, "the Claymore's a fine ship and only the severest gales would . . ."

"Which means," interrupted the Superintendent as if pursuing a continuous train of thought, "that such things as renewed vehicle excise licences could take a considerable time getting here from the mainland offices. I've no doubt, Constable McKinnon that you take this into account when considering excise prosecutions."

Calum knew then that the absence of a licence on old Duncan's van hadn't been missed by his superior. Calum was an uncomplicated man living among uncomplicated people where a spade is always a spade. This man puzzled him.

"I try to be fair," Calum faltered.

The Superintendent, who had been intently examining his lighter, raised his head and looked at Calum with more than a trace of a smile. "I didn't doubt that for a moment."

"Well Constable, I might as well have a look at your pub while I'm here," he said and turning, led the way into the saloon bar.

At this early hour in the day the bar was, as Calum expected, empty except for Ian Mor the barman behind the counter reading last week's *Oban Times*.

The sound of the Superintendent's "Good morning to you" caused Ian to hastily fold away the paper and, registering surprise at seeing Calum in uniform and looking at the stranger expectantly, he waited. Calum cleared his throat and informed

Ian that the gentleman was a Superintendent on a visit of inspection to the island.

"You'll take a dram on the house gentlemen," Ian Mor invited reaching for the glasses.

"Thank you, but no," declined the stranger politely, "not while on duty."

During the embarrassed pause that followed the Superintendent's eyes roved round the interior of the bar, coming to rest at last on a magnificent stuffed salmon in a glass case taking pride of place on the gantry. Noting the visitor's interest Ian declared it to be the biggest fish known to have been taken from the local river. Seeing that he had the gentleman's attention he went on to inform him that it weighed over 30lbs and had been caught during the war by a young lad evacuated to the island from Glasgow.

"Aye," purred Ian Mor, "a fine fish caught on a Jock Scott. And it tied by your ownself Calum, as I remember."

"Really," admired the Superintendent. "I fish a bit myself. Perhaps you would tie one for me sometime, Constable?"

When they left the bar the Superintendent led the way till they reached the shop of Alasdair McDonald—or Alasdair *Crubach* the cobbler as he was known to all, on account of a limp he had had from childhood. He bent forward, hands clasped behind his back and peered through the dusty window at some tired old shoes that had been mended but not claimed and now offered themselves, without much hope, for sale.

"One of the worst evils in the city is gambling," the Superintendent declared straightening himself and drawing back his shoulders. "So much misery it causes, broken homes and debt. I don't suppose, Constable McKinnon, that you've had the opportunity to witness the havoc it can cause."

Calum groaned inwardly at what he was hearing.

Someone must have informed on him and this man must know about his once weekly evening in Crubach's back shop with Archie the Post and Seaoaidh the Milk playing whist at a penny a point. On a bad night he'd lost as much as 50p which, although it had never caused even a sensation of misery in *his* home, it was still gambling. *Mo creach*, he'd be out of a job, and his house too.

"To be honest sir," Calum began his confession, "I must admit . . ."

But the Superintendent was already striding off in the direction of the river, apparently having lost interest in the subject. When Calum caught up with him, he was leaning far out over the bridge, a hand over his eyes against the sun, staring at the deep, dark water flowing beneath the overhanging bank.

"A first class lie for a fish wouldn't you say, Constable?" he said glancing up at Calum.

"The very spot that the big one was taken, that you saw in the pub, sir." Calum confirmed.

"Indeed?" the Superintendent enthused, returning his attention to the smoothly gliding current. "And on a Jock Scott as I recall."

They strolled uphill towards the Police Station and Calum was glad of the easier pace. The impending interview with his superior, when they reached the station and his meagre file of reports was inspected, weighed heavily on him.

How could he explain to this city man that the people on his islands were not criminals—foolish, even childish at times but not bad, no evil in them. How could he make him understand the horror felt, the lasting shame suffered by an islander taken to court on the mainland. How could a people, many of whom could barely speak far less read English, be expected to understand regulations made for city people with city ways. He could tell him of this one or that one, so many, kept from straying by a quiet word at the right time. But that would be breaking a confidence, the betrayal of trust between himself and his people which had taken years to establish.

As they were about to pass the little church the Superintendent halted and without comment he pushed open the iron gate and entered the cemetry. At the entrance Calum hesitated, casting his eye around for some act of vandalism that his superior must have spotted. Vandalism, he thought, and smiled for the first time that day. The children would have to look up a dictionary to learn what the word meant. He passed through the gate and followed the Superintendent at a short distance.

The man wandered along the rows of tombstones, pausing now and then to read an inscription and occasionally asked Calum what he knew of this family or that. One such memorial was in the form of a small marble cross. After reading the scant information given, he looked inquiringly at Calum.

"She wasn't an islander," Calum informed, "just a wee slip of a lass who came here with her older brother Jamie, from Glasgow."

The Superintendent made no comment so Calum continued. "They were staying with old Meg McDougall at the far end of the village. The war in Korea was on at the time and their father, a soldier, reported missing. When their mother, poor soul, suffered a complete breakdown and was hospitalised for an indefinite period, the children were sent here for old Meg to look after. It's the sharp tongue and short temper that was at the old one, but good enough at heart for all that.

"Och, but they were the lively ones the two children, always up to tricks. But no badness in them, you'll understand, sir.

"Well old Meg, being what she was, her and the young lad fell out one day and did he not storm out of the house taking his sister with him. The last she saw of them they were climbing up Beinn Bhreac, that hill you can see at the back of the village. Meg expected that they would be back long before tea-time. When they didn't appear and it December, she called me. I told her I'd bring them home and took to the hill."

Calum turned to stare at the hill rising sheer behind him and his face was grave.

"Did you find them?" asked the Superintendent

"Oh yes I found them all right," sighed Calum roused from his reverie. "See sir, like a gash on the cliff face, there to the right, near the summit? As I said it was in December and by the time I was half way up the hill the snow started. Just a flurry at first then heavier, thicker and the light beginning to go. I was much younger then and not long on the island. I'd only been up the hill once before and then it had been the summer. I cursed myself for not taking someone with me. With the light going and the snow in my face I couldn't see barely a yard in any direction.

"Suddenly I lost my footing and fell or rather rolled and slithered backwards down the hill. That's how I found them or, to be accurate, they found me.

"I must have lost consciousness for a moment for I remember lying on my back and their two frightened faces peering down at me. I tried to stand but my right leg wouldn't bear my weight. The lad had a thick coat and stout boots but the lass was wearing ankle-socks and wee strapover shoes and only a cardigan over her cotton dress. I wrapped her in my coat and the lad and I held her close through the night.

"I don't remember much of that night—whether I slept or just lost consciousness, I don't know. With the coming of daylight the snow stopped and we could see where we were. I tried standing and found that although my leg ached, I could move it. The little lass seemed to be asleep. She had a funny wee smile on her face like she was dreaming.

"We started off down the hill, the lad in front to test the ground and me with the lass in my arms. We hadn't gone far when the search-party met us. The doctor told me later that the wee soul must have slipped away just minutes before they found us. She wasn't strong like her brother and couldn't stand the cold.

"We buried her here in Cill-Chuimhne. The islanders keep her grave as they would one of their own."

Both stood in silence by the tiny plot. It was the Superintendent who was first to speak.

"I noticed you have a slight limp. You said you fell . . . that night on the hill."

"Och, it was just what I think they call a hair-line fracture. It mended fine but it does trouble me a bit at times and . . . I'm not so young as I was then."

When they reached the Police Station the Superintendent settled himself at Calum's desk and lit a cigarette. Calum went to the cupboard and turning, offered his report file. But the Superintendent didn't seem to notice his action.

"What happened to the boy?" he asked carefully tapping his cigarette over the ashtray.

"Young Jamie," Calum replied, his mind stretching back over the years. "Well he took his sister's death very hard, retired into himself, as it were and didn't speak much to anybody. We contacted the hospital in Glasgow at the time but were told that his mother's condition was such that she couldn't be informed about what had happened. So he stayed on at Old Meg's but things went from bad to worse between them. The schoolmaster told me that his work had fallen off badly and him one of the best scholars the master ever had."

"Understandable in the circumstances," judged the Superintendent. "What became of him subsequently?"

"One evening some time after," Calum resumed, "I was taking a foot patrol through the village. I was passing the grocer's when I heard a noise at the back of the shop. I went quietly round and was just in time to see wee Jamie's rear going through the back window. I grabbed him by the seat of his breeks and pulled him out. I still can see his wee defiant face looking up at me. Then he started to cry, softly almost to himself.

"I shut the window and took him home with me. Jean, my wife, made tea and buttered scones for us and left us sitting together by the fire. We sat for a while sipping our tea, when finally Jamie spoke.

"It wasn't for myself, Mr McKinnon. It was for my wee sister Mary." He sat looking into the fire for a while and I thought best to keep silent.

"When we were on the hill, before you found us, with all that snow we didn't know where we were and Mary was so cold and frightened. She kept asking for a sweetie and I didn't have any, Mr McKinnon. I didn't have any. I told her that, if she was a good girl and went to sleep, I'd give her a whole bag of sweets when we got home.

"The fire crackled up the chimney and such misery on his wee face I'd never seen before nor, I hope will ever see again.

"When you wrapped her in your coat she did go to sleep didn't she, Mr McKinnon? She was a good girl wasn't she, Mr McKinnon?

"Jamie seemed to gather himself together and after a

bit, he looked up at me. He wasn't crying. His face was set, determined almost challenging.

"I don't have any pocket-money, Mr McKinnon, and I know she doesn't need sweets now but . . . I promised her."

"What did you do . . . I mean about the boy?" the Superintendent asked.

"I kept him at my house after that. Fetched his things from Old Meg—she didn't really mind—too old really to look after a young lad. Jean took to him right away and he to her. You see we weren't long married and hadn't any children of our own.

"After that his school work improved and he started to play with the other lads. One evening I was going to the river to try for a fish and took him with me, felt he needed an interest. He took to fishing like a duck to water. Many's an evening we cast through the pools and many's the good fish we pulled. In the end it was Jamie who got the big one. You remember sir, the one we saw in the bar?"

The Superintendent nodded his head and rising, stepped to the window and gazed at the summit of Beinn Bhreac.

"Tell me . . . where is Jamie now?"

"I can't rightly say sir," replied Calum. "The war ended in Korea and his father, who'd been held prisoner in the north, was repatriated. He arrived here one day out of the blue. I showed him his daughter's grave then he took Jamie back home to Glasgow. I got a letter from his mother shortly after, thanking us for our trouble. Trouble—Jamie was no trouble to us. Anyway he wrote that Jamie's mother was much better and that they'd bought a flat in city. I never heard from them again."

Calum picked up the report file which he had laid on the counter and again offered it to the Superintendent.

"I don't think I need bother with that," he declined. "I'm

certain that you can keep the Queen's Peace on your island without overburdening the Inspector in Oban with too much paperwork. However I'd better sign it."

He took the file, carried it to the bar counter and with his back to Claum initialed the last page and closed the folder.

"Good Lord!" he exclaimed, "The ferry leaves in fifteen minutes. We'll have to hurry."

The Superintendent stepped on to the gangway and turned to Calum who raised his arm in salute. From his inside pocket he withdrew a brown envelope and handed it to Calum.

"You believed what the boy told you . . . about the sweets being for his sister?" he asked.

"Aye sir. Jamie wouldn't lie," Calum assured him.

"I wonder," the Superintendent said, "if there'll be a good run of fish this year. Perhaps I'll try my hand at the back end. You never know I may even get a bigger one than your Jamie, if you were to tie a fly or two for me."

Calum watched the ferry boat sail into the distance then drove back to the Police Station.

For a spell he gazed through the office window at the mist gathering on the summit of Beinn Bhreac. Then he reached for the folder that the Superintendent had initialed, to replace it in the filing cupboard. As he did so a very old, ragged Jock Scott salmon fly dropped from it on to the counter.

15

Peace Be With You, Calum

"*A mach a so, a Chaluim,*" Jean scorned her husband, Constable Calum McKinnon from his tiny office where he had been ineffectually trying to clean and bring some order into the chaos of scattered files, forms and dust-covered amendments. "Away and put the kettle on," she devised an excuse to get him out from under her feet. "Maybe you'll just about manage that."

Calum had no qualms about delegating the responsibility for the office to his good lady for over their years together on the island, she had had to compensate for his loathing of all forms of paperwork. In the kitchen he switched on the kettle. Then filling a bucket with water, he went out into the pleasantness of a spring morning to wash his patrol car. Those who were acquainted with Constable McKinnon might well have been excused if they had raised a surprised eyebrow at such a show of industry on his part.

Spring in the Western Isles is signalled when the sap begins to rise in the winter-dormant trees, sea-trout to fill the spate-browned river pools, and speckled fawns on spindly legs to browse the first dewed grass-shoots on the wooded slopes. On the mainland, on the other hand, the season is marked by a mass exodus of urban-domiciled police hierarchies from the familiar confines of their city boundaries to the wastelands reputed to lie beyond. The energy then being expended by Calum was occasioned by the imminent arrival of the Chief Constable on his annual tour of inspection.

"Properly attired in your best uniform McKinnon, you will greet the CC at your office door with a smart salute. Expected time of arrival is 2pm. Under no circumstances will you leave the office before the CC has been. Do I make myself perfectly clear, McKinnon?"

Calum had acknowledged the inspector's explicit instructions, telephoned the previous day from the mainland sub-divisional headquarters. As he replaced the receiver, Calum couldn't for the life of him fathom why the man had sounded so agitated. After all, it wouldn't be the first visit he'd had a visit from a Chief Constable.

By 1.30pm on the appointed day, Calum felt that everything was as right as it would ever be and was sitting suited in his number one uniform, sipping a cup of tea when the telephone sounded.

"I'll get it," Jean said rising quickly, fearful of the shambles that her husband could create in the office simply by answering the phone. There was concern on Jean's face when she returned.

"It's the minister, Calum," she reported, glancing anxiously at the clock on the mantlepiece. "He wants to speak to you urgently." Moments later she heard the office door close and her husband's patrol car start up. The hands of the clock stood at 1.40pm.

Exactly twenty minutes later Jean observed through the window of her living room a maroon coloured limousine draw up outside the station. With a pounding heart, she heard the crunch of footsteps on the gravel path leading to the office, followed by the summoning ring of the bell. She rose, smoothed a crease from her dress and hurried to the office. The sight which confronted her on the doorstep would have daunted a person of lesser mettle than Jean. A tall man, his uniform resplendently adorned with the highest insignia of rank, flanked on either side by uniforms only slightly less impressive, towered over her.

"Good day to you, gentlemen," Jean greeted, undecided whether to salute or curtsey. "Please come in," she invited, falling back before the advance of the official party. "The books are all there on the counter ready for your inspection. I think you'll find them in order. I'm Calum's . . . Constable McKinnon's wife and you sir, will be the Chief Constable, I'm thinking." She addressed the tall man, tentively offering her hand.

"I am indeed, Mrs McKinnon," the visitor confirmed. In stark contrast to the thunderous looks on the faces of his two companions, there was an engaging quality in the tall man's smile as he stooped to accept her proffered hand, which gave Jean some much needed encouragement. "It's always a pleasure for me to meet the wives and families of my officers . . . but we did rather expect to find your husband here when we arrived. I trust he's not ill?"

"It's kind of you to be concerned, sir. But no, he's just fine. Och, he has a touch of the rheumatism when there's dampness in it, but then there's neither of us getting any younger," Jean informed, flattered by her distinguished visitor's interest.

"Where exactly is your husband, Mrs McKinnon?" the staff officer at the CC's elbow enquired icily.

"I'm afraid I've no idea," Jean had to confess. "He had a phone call from the Reverend McPherson and went off a while ago, without saying where. He'll be that vexed when he gets back and finds he's missed you," she regretted. "Och, but not to worry, gentlemen. I can answer all your questions, for is it not myself that's well acquainted with the office and can put my hand on things far better than Calum ever could."

Moving to the desk, she pulled back the chair, inviting the CC to make himself comfortable. "I'll just slip through to the kitchen and put the kettle on and be right back. I'm sure you must all be ready for a cup of tea after your journey over from the mainland."

The evening was well advanced and the distinguished party long departed the island before Jean heard Calum's patrol car arrive back at the station and his key turn in the office door. There were a few things she had to say to her husband, the spoiled meal in the oven being the least of them. But the sight of Calum slumped in his desk chair stilled her anger.

"*A dhia*, Calum, what's happened?" she asked, her hand light on his shoulder, her voice gentle when she saw the sadness in his eyes.

"Old Donald the gamekeeper passed away an hour ago," he sighed. "It's the fine man he was, Jean. I never knew a better one." Calum felt the comforting squeeze of Jean's hand on his shoulder. "He wanted to see me before the end. That was why the minister rang." For a time there was silence between them. "I had to go, didn't I Jean, even if it meant missing the Chief Constable?" he asked, looking up at his wife for reassurance.

"Of course you did, *a ghraidh*," she answered. "You wouldn't have been the man I married if you hadn't."

There will be all hell to pay when the Inspector learns, as he surely will, that I wasn't here to receive them," Calum prophesised. "Maybe even the sack."

"Would that be so awful?" Jean wondered, but the question was more in her mind than on her lips. Never by a word had he betrayed himself but for some time past her woman's intuition had sensed a restlessness in her husband. And increasingly she had found him gazing vacantly into space for long periods at a time, lost to the world around. "Come on, Calum. I'll make us something to eat," Jean said finally. "We'll let tomorrow look after itself."

Jean's optimism concerning the morrow proved unfounded for, barely had they finished their meal, than the telephone shrilled in the office.

"You have your smoke, Calum. I'll answer it," she said, determined, if at all possible, to allow her husband time to settle his thoughts.

"It's your inspector," she reported reluctantly. "He insists on speaking to you."

"I can imagine he does," Calum replied, rising wearily to his feet.

Calum's absence seemed an eternity to Jean as she waited anxiously in the kitchen.

"What did he have to say?" she asked when he returned silently to his chair, sucking on his empty pipe.

"A great deal to be sure, and most of it not fit to be

repeated," Calum replied, reaching for his tobacco-pouch. "I've to cross to the mainland the day after tomorrow on the early ferry and be in his office at 9am sharp."

"What's to happen then, Calum?" Jean worried.

"Och, somebody high up, who's in charge of discipline—a Deputy Chief Constable I think he is—is coming to . . ." Calum managed a rueful grin, " . . . attend to me, as the inspector was pleased to term it."

"But didn't you tell the Inspector why you were away from the station?" Jean queried.

"I had half a mind to but I couldn't get a word in with him going on and on about neglect of duty and disgracing the uniform and then he just hung up—probably ran out of breath, I'm thinking. You know, Jean," he added seriously, "I don't belive that man likes me all that much."

"They shouldn't be doing this to you, Calum. It wasn't your fault you weren't here." Jean was angry. "When you tell them where you were, and why . . ."

"I wasn't where I was supposed to be and that will be that," Calum declared with a finality that brooked no contradiction. "I just hope he doesn't take all day over it, so I can get back in time for Donald's funeral."

Much of the following day Calum spent closeted in his office. Regularly Jean took cups of coffee through to him and always she found him leafing through old files of instructions and reports that hadn't seen the light of day for years. The wastepaper-basket, she observed, was filled to overflowing. When her husband's brows were down, as they were then, Jean knew not to bother him but at last she simply had to know what on earth he was doing.

"Clearing the decks, *a graidh*," was his explanation. "Just clearing the decks."

That evening Calum did less than justice to the meal Jean had prepared. He picked at the food but his mind seemed to be elsewhere. Once or twice she had the feeling that he was about to say something important to her, but even as quickly he would retreat back into himself and the moment was lost. Neither of them slept much that night.

The early morning, a pale promise of a fine day to come, found Calum once again attired in his number one uniform boarding the ferry for the mainland. He had little to say to Jean before taking his leave other than requiring that his Sunday suit be left out. For come what may, he intended to be present in the little stone-walled cemetery by the shore when Old Donald was laid to rest.

In the mainland sub-divisional office where Calum might have expected a welcome from old colleagues, he had the distinct impression that he had become a known carrier of an infectious disease. The mere sight of him was sufficient to send passing staff members and even grizzled, grey-haired sergeants scuttling for cover, almost as if he had a notice pinned to his tunic bearing the legend, Unclean.

"Constable McKinnon has arrived, sir," the bar-officer informed the Inspector on the telephone. "Yes sir, right away sir." He gingerly replaced the receiver. "He wants to see you in his office immediately," the bar-officer hurriedly passed on the dreaded summons, as if needing to rush to the washroom to gargle with several glassfuls of strong antiseptic, least even the forming on his lips of the name, McKinnon, might prove fatal.

Calum's knock on the inspector's door received a perfunctory invitation to "Come". Stationing himself before his superior's desk, he was obliged to wait, his presence ignored, while the inspector carefully read over and appended his signature to several, seemingly important documents.

Calum's eyes strayed round the walls of the room where hung framed photographs of its previous occupiers. Some few he had known and respected, others he had just known. He wondered where the present incumbent would choose to position his portrait when the time came? He had just decided that directly over the waste-bin would be a suitable site when his deliberation was interrupted by the inspector's mono-syllabic injunction, "Sit". Calum sat.

"Aware as I am, McKinnon, of your total ignorance of the various forms currently in use in this force, I have personally selected the one appropriate to your present situation," the inspector advised, indicating with tap of the rubbered end of his pencil, a document which he had placed squarely on the blotter in front of him. "It is form number 1:28:1. As this information will have absolutely no significance to you, I will explain its purpose in one simple word . . . Resignation." The Inspector sat back in his chair and bestowed on Calum the tolerant smile that a long suffering parent would on an errant but not very bright child.

"I have filled in all the relevant details and it now requires only your signature. The Deputy Chief Constable will be with us shortly and although I can promise you nothing, McKinnon, I'm certain that your resignation on my desk would go a long way towards improving your position regarding the pension."

The Inspector extracted from his tunic pocket an expensive fountain pen—a birthday present from his adoring wife—and with deliberation and evident satisfaction, he unscrewed the top before offering it to Calum.

Whether Calum would have accepted the proffered instrument of his abdication or not will for ever remain a matter of conjecture, for at that moment there was a knock on the door, swiftly followed by the appearance of the bar-officer, stiffly at attention, to announce the arrival of the Deputy CC. Simultaneously Calum and the inspector sprang to their feet.

The arrival was above middle height, greying at the temples and dressed in a sombrely dark civilian suit of quality cut. Calum's spirits, already at a low ebb, plunged to zero as he passively witnessed the Inspector shake hands with the Deputy and exchange pleasantries. The Inspector surrendered his desk to the VIP and settled himself on a side chair with a notepad open on his knee and pen poised, ready to record every last detail of the final downfall and humiliation of the pestilential Constable Calum McKinnon.

"I would prefer to see Constable McKinnon on my own if you don't mind, Inspector." The Deputy's tone was conversational but the implied suggestion that the Inspector had a choice as to go or remain was clearly a polite formality.

"But . . . but of course, just as you wish, sir," the Inspector experienced some difficulty getting his words out as he struggled to his feet, dropping and picking up his pad in the process. "I'll be in the next room . . . . er . . . when you want me," he advised, closing the door behind him.

For a little the Deputy studied Calum from behind the desk then rising, he extended his hand. "I'm sorry that we should meet under such unhappy circumstances, Mr McKinnon."

In the adjacent room the inspector paced the floor like an expectant father. Each time he reached the door that separated him from a scene he had often imagined he paused to listen. But from the other side of the solid oak door he could discern not so much as a murmur. He was about to begin his umteenth circuit when the door was thrown open and the Deputy, closely followed by Calum, emerged.

"Would you be so kind, Inspector, as to order a car to take us to the pier," the Deputy requested.

To suggest that the Inspector's conception of the world crumbled, would be something of an exaggeration . . . but only just. Surely the worthy, in whose ranks he naturally numbered himself, were rewarded; and the worthless, among whom Constable McKinnon surely stood shoulder high, received their just desserts?

Rational articulaton being quite beyond him, the Inspector directed the execution of the Deputy's wishes by a vague flapping of his hand in the general direction of an attendant sergeant. He was able only to stare dumbly at the dignified figure of his intended victim depart the sacrificial altar, leaving him with his priestly blade unblooded.

In a shaded corner of the little stone-walled cemetery by the shore, Calum and the Deputy helped lower with silken cords the mortal remains of Old Donald the gamekeeper into his grave. They bowed their heads while the minister spoke the eulogy. When the other mourners had drifted off the two tarried a little by the mound of earth which would shortly cover for ever someone whom they had both, unknown to each other, loved and respected.

"My father was in the regular army and away most of the time," the Deputy chose to explain. "Old Donald, he was an uncle on my mother's side, raised me as a boy here on the island. Those were happy days for me. I didn't see much of him after I married and settled down but we did correspond regularly."

"He was the first friend I made when I came here and me ready to put the world to rights," Calum recalled. "Thank God I had enough sense to listen to his advice. If I hadn't I wouldn't have lasted six months on this island."

With the sound of the ceaseless ebb and flow of the sea across the shingle in their ears, they wandered towards the gate.

"You were often mentioned in his letters," the Deputy said. "And from what he wrote I know he had a high regard for you, in and out of uniform.

"I was in London when the minister phoned the news of his sudden illness to my home but by the time it reached me, it was too late." The Deputy paused at the gate and turned to face Calum. "I can't say how much I regret not being with him but it is a comfort to know that he had good friends by him at the last."

On the drive back to the pier the Deputy broached the subject which he knew must still be causing his constable some anxiety.

"I explained to the Chief Constable the reason for your absence when he called at your station and he asked me to inform you that, in the circumstances, you got your priorities right."

The following morning Calum sat back at the desk in his tiny office and gazed through the window at the fishing boats in the harbour below, rising and gently falling with the coming tide. In his mind he pictured the crews, the night's catch of herring being discharged, asleep in the fo'c'sle, dead to the smell of warm diesel from the adjoining engineroom. It had all been so familiar to him as a youth on his father's boat and not for the first time he wondered about his life and what it might have been. So occupied was he indeed with his thoughts, that he was unaware of his wife's presence until roused by the clink of a cup and saucer being placed on the bar counter.

"A penny for them, Calum," she said.

"Och, I was just thinking, Jean," he answered sipping his hot coffee, "it's a while now since we've been home."

"I thought this was home," she countered.

"Well it is, in a manner of speaking," he admitted. "But we'll have to move out of here when I retire . . . which I can do at any time, now that I've got my twenty five in."

"I suppose you could," she conceded wondering where the conversation was leading.

"The croft house was looking in good order the last time we were over," Calum mentioned, "and would it not be with my cousin Archie keeping his eye on it over the years?"

"You know, Jean," he continued as if an idea had suddenly occurred to him. "What with grants and the likes, it wouldn't cost all that much to build on a fine big kitchen."

"A woman certainly needs a bit of elbow-room in her kitchen," Jean was only too ready to agree.

"And double glazing for the windows wouldn't be a bad thing either," he added.

"That too," she nodded, carried on the current of her husband's enthusiasm.

"Cousin Archie manages well enough, wouldn't you say, with a sheep or two on the hill and what he makes at the prawn fishing," Calum suggsted.

"He doesn't go short," she opinioned, "and was it not draining his land he was at the last time we were there?"

"There'd be grants for that too," Calum judged, "and maybe something towards buying a boat. There's one for sale in Oban right now that would do just grand, and enough creels to make a start."

Jean studied her husband as he spoke—the eagerness in his voice, the excitement in his eyes, the qualities in him which had first attracted her those many years ago and absent for so long. He so reminded her, just then, of a huge black stallion she'd seen when a girl back in her village.

Try as they might they could never quite break his spirit. A moment's inattention on the part of the ploughman and he'd be off, the traces snapped, heading for the hill and freedom. In her heart of hearts Jean knew what was in her husband's mind and that he needed only a word from her.

"I'd want a brand new cooker," she said decisively, "none of your second hand rubbish, mind you."

Calum was on his feet in an instant with poor Jean enfolded in his bear's hug, gasping for breath. "The best thing that money can buy, *a ghraidh*," he vowed. After more than two decades of obedient service—or as near as his nature had allowed—Calum McKinnon was his own man again.

"I wonder now," Calum puzzled as he grinned down at the flushed face of his wife. "What was the number of that form the Inspector wanted me to sign when I was in his office yesterday?"

For the first time, as Calum's unpaid secretary, Jean neither knew nor cared.

THE END